NVA - North Vietnamese Army

GI - Soldiers of the US Army

VC - Viet Cong, name given to opposition in the South

ARVN - Army Republic of Viet Nam. South Vietnamese Army

USARV - US Army Republic Viet Nam

PHOENIX PROGRAM - US run assassination program in the South

HOOCH - Generic name for rustic GI housing

AWOL - Absent without leave

OFF LIMITS - Areas in which American soldiers were not allowed

DUST OFF - Helicopters that rescued wounded from the Tield

HUEY - Helicopter synonymous with Viet Nam War

REMF - Troops that lived in the rear

MACV - Military Assistance Command Vietnam

BOQ - Bachelor officer quarters

TDY - Temporary duty assignment

CHOLON - Chinese city adjacent to Saigon

DMZ - Border between North and South Vietnam

R&R - Rest and recuperation leave granted to Vietnam soldiers

LZ - Helicopter battlefield landing zone

CO - Commanding Officer

NCO - Non-commissioned Officer

APC - Armored Personnel Carrier

The Girl

from

Tam Hiep

A NOVEL FROM THE WAR

John W. Conroy

The Girl from Tam Hiep
Copyright 2021 by John W. Conroy

ISBN: 978-1-09837-167-8 (print)
ISBN: 978-1-09837-168-5 (eBook)

Cover design by KC Reiter
Cover photos by John W Conroy
Press information conroyvn@gmail.com

Screenplay available

CHAPTER 1

THERE was no movement within the hooch. The voice of the General droned on from a radio somewhere inside. "…every soldier in Vietnam will have, on this Christmas Day, a hot meal of roast turkey, mashed potatoes, and all the fixings. From Ca Mau to the demilitarized zone (DMZ)…from Cam Ranh Bay to Loc Ninh, a hot traditional Christmas dinner will be served to every American. Our boys fighting this war deserve no less."

This hooch was actually a tent set up over a floor made of pierced steel planking (PSP). Two rows of army cots lined either side. Some had mosquito nets draped over them. Others were bare. There was the belief among some of the men that the nets held the heat, that overpowering, oppressive heat, which was always present in this part of Vietnam, except for early in the morning before dawn, when a blanket was needed. There were foot lockers and wall lockers, many of which were homemade, between the bunks. Empty beer cans, whisky bottles, spent roaches, and scorched opium pipes from Christmas Eve littered the planking. PX fans turned slowly at either end.

I had returned late on Christmas Eve from Bien Hoa, after the curfew, lying on the floor of a Lambretta to avoid the military police (MPs). It had been quieter than usual, especially since the curfew had been changed from 10 a.m. to 6 p.m. I'd been looking for Kim Lon. Not that I expected to see her in town, but once she had shown up at "The Black Rose," a soul brother bar. She was a dark-skinned girl from Cambodia. Not Ebony, not dusky… but that dark hue beyond the golden bronze so common to the native girls of Vietnam.

The radio suddenly turned silent and was replaced by a voice from the rear of the hooch.

"There…pulled the plug on that motherfucker. The last thing I need is a fucking turkey. Why doesn't he 'personally' end this fucking war?"

"Are you actually considering the possibility that he could, or that he would?" I said, in answering PFC Bobby D Banks, direct from the hills of Arkansas. "Go back to sleep. This day may have the potential to stretch way beyond that turkey dinner. But first I need some rest after the late ride back last night."

Silence returned to the hooch. A silence itself that was notable for the lack of the sound of a Huey. No hint of a helicopter in the distance, and we didn't live that far from the 93rd Evacuation Hospital's chopper pad that was ordinarily busy twenty-four hours a day.

I retreated to the mosquito net that draped over the cot, my refuge from the lives of others. Kim Lon returned to my thoughts. She walked fast and held herself so straight though she wasn't tall. She was a quiet beauty with a shy smile. Everything but her feet that looked as if they'd trailed a water buffalo through the paddy for a hundred years, while she was barely eighteen, so she claimed.

An orange glow from the eastern sky began to penetrate the lower edge of the PSP. You just knew the smoke from the shit burning details was beginning to spread throughout the Company area. Nothing, however, could obscure the beauty of a sunrise in this mysterious land. By now, the upper arch of the sun would be climbing over the horizon of the western edge of the South China Sea, from the sands along the beaches at Vung Tau, making invisible the scars of the bombs, the sprays, and the napalm.

Mail call was beginning so why not check for a Christmas card with some cash tucked away inside. Bob and I were heading up the line. Neither of us had checked for a few days. Contact from that other world was beginning to matter less and less. But as we were both broke, there was always the chance. Hell, it was Christmas morning, and there wasn't an evergreen in sight.

"I'll tell you something, Collins" drawled Bobby D. "Not much of a chance that anyone from my clan is going to remember me on Christmas, much less send money. I don't really stay in touch."

I did write, and some from my family had already sent cards along with a few gifts.

"Maybe mine will" I answered, "but it wouldn't be much. They're a frugal bunch."

The mail clerk swung open the Conex that served as a company post office.

"Here we go, boys. Let's see if any of you assholes have a family or a friend back in the world; someone who remembers you're over here fighting for their freedom."

Names were read off. Cards, letters, packages were handed out. The last one, "PFC Bill Collins."

It was from my old Aunt Alice, a retired librarian, and there was a "green" five-dollar bill tucked inside. A five from Baltimore, and since US green was forbidden in Vietnam, under pain of death, some said because of the rampant inflation that was ruining the country's economy, it was worth twice that on the black market. American personnel in Vietnam were paid with military pay certificates (MPC), which according to the rules should be changed into VN Piasters before being spent locally, but who the hell would do that? Throw away good money. Let the government do it.

"Well, it's a start," said Bob.

"And a finish," said I. "No other possibilities. Let's see how far it'll go. And fuck that turkey. Westmoreland can shove them all up his ass as far as I'm concerned, right along with the mashed potatoes and the cranberries… right along with this war."

"What about Santimaw?" asked Bob. 'Larry's gonna be pissed if we don't take him along."

"Well, hell, he's broke too, and there's hardly enough here for the two of us."

"Just asking," said Bob.

Traffic on the Bien Hoa–Saigon highway was especially light. The US Army was sleeping late this Christmas morning, as apparently were the Viet Cong (VC). A truce had been called for Christmas Day, and let's hope that included the MPs. We'd both be AWOL (absent without official leave), like usual.

Still no Hueys choppering into the 93rd Evac. landing pad. None either just north at II Field Force Headquarters or northeast on the grounds of the 199th Light Infantry Brigade. It looked like a boring Christmas for those who chose it and more so to those in the field who received it as a gift.

Tam Hiep beckoned for it was the closest to the wire, and the home of Kim Lon; however, it had been off limits for some time and was too chancy during daylight hours. The MPs were afraid of the night in this supposedly VC town, which lay just beyond the western edge of Route #1-A.

Crossing over this highway was at times more dangerous than a night out on ambush or listening posts. There were army deuce-and-a-half's, five quarters, jeeps, five tons, ten tons, armored personnel carriers (APCs), and everything else army green. The outer lane packed with local traffic comprised motorbikes, three-wheeled Lambrettas, bicycles, Citrons from the thirties and forties that were the local Bien Hoa buses, along with the occasional ox cart hoping for one more successful trek without being run over by the Green Machine.

After a safe crossing, it was down the path through the trench and into the shacks and frog ponds beyond. We were taking the shortcut along the fringe of Tam Hiep to the Bien Hoa highway. Most of the residents here were women, for the men and the boys were off in one army or the other. Many of these girls worked inside the wire for the US Military. A rather odd setup when one considers that USARV (US Army Republic Vietnam) in its infinite wisdom had them all pegged as VC.

On this Christmas morning, we decided on Bien Hoa, which lay a few miles to the west. We'd pass on the highway through Tam Hiep and Tan Mai, to the old provincial capital whose days of past glory were unknown to the American GI. When the French ruled Indochina, this sleepy town on the placid Dong Nai River had been a destination for Saigon café society, an escape from the sultry, humid evenings of that city. They would have traveled up old colonial route one, the original and only highway that connected Phnom Penh with Hanoi, threading its way from the Cambodian border through the whole of Vietnam. The Bien Hoa–Saigon portion was still the best way for discreet trips to and from Saigon for it was hardly ever traveled by MPs. In the late fifties, the American company Morrison-Knudson had built the more direct Route 1-A between Saigon and Long Binh.

"So where to now, Collins?" said Bob. "What all's your Santa cash from back in the world gonna be buying us? Some pussy, I hope. And maybe some good bourbon."

We were in a Lambretta just passing the concrete water tower under construction by an Australian Company near the gates to the US Air Base at Bien Hoa. The military traffic here as on the main highway was light to nonexistent; however, the locals were out having coffee, pho, or an early beer as was their custom.

Christmas was no big deal in this Buddhist country, though an exception could be made for Ho Nai, a few miles north, which had been settled by Catholics from North Vietnam before the final partitioning in 1956. "The Blessed Virgin has gone South" went the CIA propaganda campaign of those times, to provide a base for the present government that was run primarily by Catholics from the North. Another odd state of affairs, but then what wasn't here?

"I think we'll do all right. The 'Hope Bar' is coming up, and it doesn't look as if they've got any business to speak of."

"Dung Lai poppa-san, Dung fucking Lai," yelled Bob at the driver. The man pulled over and accepted fifty cents MPC as we jumped clear, him wishing it was more from his expression but glad to be rid of us nonetheless.

"I don't know how we'll do here," said Bob. "With the cash, I mean. Those airborne grunts from the 173rd ruin the prices."

"Yea, but the girls know we're locals. It'll be OK."

This easygoing joint on the eastern fringe of the city was the hangout of the 173rd Airborne Brigade that was headquartered on the air base nearby. When they were in from the field, they threw their cash around without much regard. They had a certain resentment toward soldiers who weren't Airborne, and much worse toward REMFs (rear echelon motherfuckers), which we were.

A bar girl approached and motioned toward a booth. There were such lovely young women here in this somewhat-sordid establishment, many of whom were of mixed blood. You could see in their faces—the French, the German, and the Senegalese—residue from that earlier war in Indo China, soon to be replaced by our own.

A girl approached. "Take a seat, GIs," she said. And to me, "I know you, GI. My friend me."

"It's Bill Collins, Kanh. This is my friend Bob. How about a couple of 33 beers…and maybe a girl for him…and teas for each of you."

Kanh was the brains of the outfit and very nice looking. The girl she brought over to sit with Banks was absolutely beautiful, and obviously "residue" from the previous conflict.

"This my friend, Tam," said Kanh. "She have French father."

"I love Tam already," said Bob.

"I love them both, but we'd better settle up on a value for the greenback before we get into any real bargaining."

Kanh thought for a minute as she looked over the money.

"This pay for the beer, the Saigon Tea, and I give you ten dollar MPC," she said.

That sounded fair enough, so after a short visit, we drank up, bid farewell to the girls, and headed out along the main drag toward downtown Bien Hoa, which was somewhat bloated with refugees from the bombing, along with the usual bars and food stalls that catered to the military. There's a native market place down along the Dong Nai River where the Bien Hoa Club is located. And there's more. Take the first right after the water tower, and you'll find the local MP lockup. So far, so good as far as that goes.

"So why didn't we stay and make a deal with those two?" asked Bobby D. "We ain't gonna find much better…anywhere. I can tell you that. Man, they both looked hot pussy."

"Right, and they both know it. You won't buy either of them off cheap and very likely not at all. You'd have to court them."

"Short time girls! You're crazy. I don't court girls back home. I just ask 'em if they wanna fuck."

"Yea, but that's Arkansas. You'd be surprised, but this place does on occasion require a certain degree of finesse."

"Well, I ain't finesse. I'm a regular 'good old boy' from the South."

"Forget it, Bob, let's get moving."

Jesus…I wonder sometimes where people are coming from. At least, he didn't shoot back with a "I ain't courtin' no whore." I've never been to Arkansas, but I've got to someday. He has expressions that blow a northerner's mind.

I was thinking how Christmas was going back in the States, but not that much. After adjusting to the routine life here in the "Green Machine," this fight for survival was taking over. The real opposition to guys like Banks and me were the US Army and their MPs. The locals were still a question mark, and we seemed to share Tam Hiep with the VC. Memories of the homefront were receding.

We flagged down another Lambretta but had second thoughts considering the cash on hand.

"Oh hell, let's walk," said Banks. "We've got all day, or have you got some kind of duty tonight?"

The only regular all-night work was routine guard duty on the perimeter. Since the ammo dump was blown a couple of weeks back, various ambush patrols and listening posts had become somewhat regular in the jungle and abandoned rubber plantations surrounding it on the beginning of the highway to Vung Tau. It was within rifle shot of the 90th Replacement Co., where most GIs entered and left the country, and which occasionally engaged in firefights with those patrols. However, the country east of the ammo dump reaching many klicks to Xuan Loc was empty and completely VC territory. It was from here that they set their mines, hid snipers, and held out with occasional brief firefights with our listening posts and ambush sites.

"No, I'm good. Looks like a free day. We need some food and some beer for starts. Let's pull in at the stall down on the market. A duck dinner is 30p (piasters). Beer's the same."

"Hey, Bob, you heard about Sparks?" It just occurred to me that we hadn't mentioned this poor guy who had been shot in the face a couple of nights ago while on a listening post by another GI who had been careless with his M-14. Someone too quick on the trigger after a sniper winged in a couple of shots that missed. Poor old Sparks would by now be "bagged and tagged" and on his way back home, much too late for Christmas. Isn't that fucked up? His poor people.

It was too bad that Santimaw wasn't with us. Larry was a wise ass, a punk kid from Sacramento but enjoyable company, and he had a good heart…and was no "lifer" I was thinking. Maybe next time.

"What you want eat, GI?" said the waitress, another beautiful specimen. "You want beer?"

"A 33 beer and a duck," said Bob. "Make that for two."

"You talk number ten 'hucking' thou, GI. You go."

"No. no," shot back Bob, "I want duck, not love…quack, quack, and it flies. We buy here before."

"Ah," said the girl. "I understand. OK, two duck and some beer. I think before, you talk bad."

I was thinking that language is quite a trip. They can't say their "f's" here, among other letters, which is confusing at times. But then again, most of the young people and especially the kids know a great deal of English, even tho' the pronunciation is usually off. When you think of it, most of us can't speak any Vietnamese; period. And you wonder about those at the top. You wonder who's translating for them, other than the girls from Tam Hiep!

We left the market and walked down the street passing the East Hotel that housed the boudoir of Miss Mai who without a doubt was the reigning queen of sexual notoriety in Bien Hoa, perhaps even the whole of South Vietnam. So, it was between there and the Dong Nai River where a cyclo driver steered us into a cheapo short time house. We were down to 450 piasters, and the going rate for a short time was 300.

"I don't know Collins. We're going to need at least 50p to make it back."

"Yea, but it's nearly the end of the month. Let's see."

The mamasan running this quaint little house was all smiles and mentioned that she had a couple of girls for 200p each. Seemed reasonable enough but only for this time and place. I wasn't any expert around women quite frankly; I was a fucked-up green in reality, but over here, girls were available most everywhere. There were car washes along most highways that were traveled by GIs, and the funny thing was, they never washed cars, or trucks. They'd start, "You want coke, you want beer, you want short time." Never, "Do you want your truck washed?" And there were no cars in this man's army, at least not north of Saigon. But "Truck Wash," that wouldn't fly.

And to be fair, I never met a girl who would have been in this line of work if it hadn't been for the war. In a ruined country with a ruined economy, whoring was one sure way of supporting the family. You've got to remember that nearly all the men were in one army or the other. Considering that with half a million "Yanks" in country, any pretty girl with a family to feed had no problem staying busy.

"Let's go for it," said Banks.

The back room had a couple of plank beds with a sheet strung on a wire between them. Par for the course for short time houses here. The girls came in, and I guess you could say we got to it. Banks swept back the sheet so he could talk as he was pumping away on the girl. Looking at him; I'd never thought of doing it this way before. He had the poor girl's heels tucked way up behind her ears as he was going at her. Looked OK, but the girls were quiet, just funny noises. They'd usually babble along with each other during the action, not paying that much attention to the customer. Once I was with a young woman who had to stop for a minute to nurse a crying baby. You got used to those kinds of things. Normality in this time and place took on another meaning.

Soon thereafter, we made our departures and began hoofing it up the street.

"You know, Banks, those girls were awfully quiet. They usually jabber away with each other, if not trying out speech with us."

"Oh, hell, I've had them light up a cigarette if I took too long," said Banks. "I've got to admit that I never seen that back home."

"Most everything I've seen here, I never saw back home; but they were awfully quiet."

"Are you for real?" asked Banks. "You didn't pick up on it?"

"How so?"

"You gotta be kidding me. You didn't fucking get it?"

"Please…tell me."

"Those poor fucking girls were deaf mutes. Why do you think they only cost 200p?"

I thought about that on the Lambretta ride back home. It didn't seem right somehow, but then again even deaf mutes need to make a living. Especially over here. They're all feeding at least one family. It's a great world we live in.

9

Banks and I made the run back with no complications. No MPs, not much traffic. The driver even seemed happy with the 50p.

We checked in at the mess hall back at the company area. The turkey and the mashed potatoes were all gone.

CHAPTER 2

A week later, we're looking at another turkey dinner…and another day off. It's not Sunday afternoon, the usual time of leisure; but let's face it, most of the lifers were heavy drinkers on a normal night, so for New Year's Eve, forget it. Not much life in the company area this morning; period. I figured I might just skip out and thumb it down to Saigon…look up an old friend from home.

It's quiet, all the way to the main gate. I looked over toward Tam Hiep, thinking a change of mind might be in the works but did not reconsider, even though Kim Lon was likely home this morning. Among her other jobs, she did laundry for the troops. She also worked as a hooch girl a few tents down from mine, and I'd stop to shoot the breeze whenever possible.

She was much more out front than the average Vietnamese girl. Not so private. She just enjoyed life. In this part of the world, a girl of twelve could run the household and the family business, and Kim was a grown woman at eighteen who knew five languages but had hardly been in a school room and was responsible for her father who lived in Phnom Penh. Every month, she'd make a run over with money for him.

It was difficult to determine if she had any romantic entanglements, either local or GI. We were only casual at this point, but I was beginning to fall for her. I fell for them all. And then there she was, humping a load of laundry across the road.

"Kim!" I yelled, "Wait up." She was carrying two huge bags of laundry on one of those sticks across her shoulders that was heavy for a GI much less a five-feet hooch girl. She stopped on the shoulder of the Tam Hiep road.

"Hey, GI…my friend you," she said, and I spoke back with, "Kim, it's Bill Collins. Bill…I hope you haven't forgotten me."

"I no forget you," she said. "You look Hollywood."

That was a stretch, but one that I gladly accepted. "Kim, would you mind if I walk along with you down to your place in Tam Hiep?"

"No, no, no, Kim Lon very busy today. Must have laundry finish for tomorrow morning. Other time for sure." I told her there was no way I'd forget and that perhaps next week things would work out. We headed off in different directions, she to Tam Hiep and me down the road toward Saigon.

The first deuce-and-a-half that came along pulled over, and I jumped in the back. It looked to be a refreshing ride. While passing the docks at Cogido along the Dong Nai River, I noticed a couple of barges loaded with pallets of ammo. Hauling them back to the Long Binh Ammo Dump with a five-ton trailer was a good job that popped up occasionally.

"Where in Saigon are you heading too?" I asked the driver. "Tan Son Nhut," he said.

That was going to work for me. Paul Savage, my old friend from the farm country, was stationed at 69 Dong Da St. in Gia Dinh, not far from the airport. He was a photo interpreter with the 4th Military Intelligence Battalion, who sometimes was TDY (Temporary Duty Assignment) with the 25th. Infantry in Cu Chi twenty miles or so NW of the airport along Route 1 toward Cambodia.

"You see that," said the driver. "That F-4 diving down on that shack along the paddy west of the highway?"

I looked over just in time to see a cannister of napalm tumbling from the F-4, going through the roof. The place erupted into flames, and no one escaped, so you had to figure a dead family who may or may not have been VC. Either way, many new recruits for the National Liberation Front (NLF). Happy New Year, Vietnam.

It all reminded me of my first trip up this highway from Camp Alpha at Ton Son Nhut to the 90th Replacement in Long Binh. Someone asked, "Why the wire mesh over the windows?"

"So the gooks can't throw a grenade inside and blow your ass away, that's why," said the driver. "Don't they know we're here to help them?" someone said. "A week here and you'll know that's a crock of shit," came the reply. "Most of them hate our fucking guts." He was right on, that driver, as far as it went.

That memory and the bombing left a bad taste in my mouth, but the mood improved as we crested the Newport Bridge that spanned the Saigon River on entry to the city. The skyline, low as it was, cleared my head, and Tu Do street beckoned if I was able to touch base with Paul. I didn't care to hoof around town on my own.

As luck would have it, the driver dropped me off at 69 Dong Da with a "Happy New Year" farewell. Paul was walking out the gate as I approached it.

"Where the hell did you show up from?" he said as he grabbed my arm.

"I thumbed down to see what's going on with you," I answered. He told me he was on his way to go flirt with girls in the coffee shop down the street. We decided to go back inside so I could check out his compound, which looked more like a hotel to me, along with a restaurant and a rooftop bar. Quite different from the tents in Long Binh.

"So this is headquarters' company for the 4th Military Intelligence Battalion MACV (U.S. Military Assistance Command, Vietnam)."

"Can't beat it," said Paul. "This makes living at home appear rough." He can say that again I was thinking. This set up would also really piss off the grunts in the field. A cousin of mine stationed up above Hue with the 1st Cav. certainly would be. He'd be right back on the REMF talk, "That those bastards get it all and we get nothing."

After the Company tour, we were back out the gate and flagged a motor cyclo for the ride downtown. Not so much traffic down this way either. We trucked down by the entrance to the airport, and I shared a joint with Paul, even though our preference was for bourbon and coke or just a cold beer. This was a hot country after all.

After stopping along the street that bordered on the recently rebuilt presidential palace to shoot a few pictures, we passed the Notre Dame cathedral and the Continental Hotel. The driver stopped, and we jumped out near the Rex Hotel, now a Bachelor Officers Quarters (BOQ), a United Service Organizations (USO) and the site of the infamous "Five O'clock Follies." All we were looking for was a hamburger from the USO. You couldn't find that on the streets. Paul talked all the way in. He was a talker. His many girl-friends back in the States had been gradually fading away. Even the main one who he had hoped would marry him after his tour here was rapidly fading.

"She's probably found some draft-dodging asshole," he was saying. "Some prick whose old man had some pull with the draft board and doesn't give fuck all about this war to begin with. Of course, neither do I."

"Well, I'll tell you something. Right now, back home, we'd probably just be leaving the milk shed after morning milking. And instead, here we are in downtown Saigon, the center of the world, in the middle of the biggest story in the world, and it didn't cost us a damn cent to get here. And as soon as we get our burgers, we'll be off down Tu Do street looking for some of the prettiest girls in the world to have a drink with. How the hell can you beat that, and we're being paid to be here."

"Yea," said Paul. "You're right. Fuck 'em all."

"And always remember, there are no cows to milk in this man's army."

You know it depends how you look at it. I didn't have any girls back home and here they were all over the place. And then there was Kim Lon back in Tam Hiep. It all seemed very promising to me. So we picked up our hamburgers, which weren't so hot but OK, and headed across the square to Tu Do St. for a beer to wash it down with.

"I don't know all the joints here," said Paul. "Been up in Cu Chi half the time since moving in and don't know the downtown here so well, you know what I mean. There's not much going on up there. We've got a detachment that works with the 25th Infantry, but up there, it's up in a Bird Dog or out in the field with the troops. Interesting, but you've gotta watch it. You can't beat living at headquarters in Saigon, that's for sure." I had to agree with him.

A couple of white chicks were entering the Caravelle Hotel as we approached but didn't give us the slightest notice. Let's face it, a couple of privates in the US Army aren't worth looking at from their perspective. Maybe if we were officers, or even better, some Harvard or Yale guy working with the State Department. You didn't see that type in the ranks for the most part, that's for sure.

"They can go fuck themselves too," said Paul. "Who needs them? I'm starting to like the local girls better. At least they pretend to like you...and some really do. I know bullshit when I see it."

We walked down past the Air France office a few blocks and stopped in at the Gala Bar at 8 Ngo Duc Ke Street just off Tu Do that joined to the traffic circle at the end of Hai Ba Trung St. along the river. It wasn't that busy or that well-lit. A girl was visible at the end of the bar reading *Paris Match* so she must speak French. I eased my way over and tried to get a conversation going.

"So what are you reading?" I started with despite knowing the magazine.

"You cannot read the cover?" she replied. "It's French."

"Just a little…my name is Bill," I answered. "How about your name?"

"Linh, my name is Linh, and you can cut the Pidgeon English. I speak it well."

Well, I thought. What's this?

Up close near the window, I could see that she was beautiful, slim with long black hair and that classic Vietnamese image and not so young. Maybe late twenties rather than the teenagers who held down most of these jobs. I was hoping that she wasn't too jaded…or too sophisticated, tho' that hadn't been the problem over here thus far, not like back in the world. However, upon recent consideration, for me, Vietnam was more and more becoming the real world.

I'm thinking how to get on with this woman. She's more than the country girls back in Tam Hiep. "So, Linh, how long have you been working in this joint?"

"What do you mean joint? I don't know that," she answered. We finally sorted out where we were, and she said that she'd been working here part time since her husband had been killed. He'd been flying a Skyraider for the ARVN Air Force when it was shot down. She's working here to support herself and her young son. Teaching French in the local schools is not enough to make ends meet.

"Ever since the Americans come to Vietnam, it costs too much to stay alive. This government does not spend much on widow pensions or on schoolteacher salaries." Then she volunteered, "I work here during the day only, and I only talk to the GIs. No more."

In the meantime, Paul had struck up a conversation with a girl at the end of the bar. "Well, Linh, how about I buy you a tea, and beers for me and my friend…and also a tea for the girl he's talking with."

She ordered up and went back to reading her French magazine. Not knowing a great deal of French, I looked along with her, at the pictures mostly, then noticed a Sean Flynn byline on a VN war picture and article. I'd read that this son of Errol was working here as a photographer. She noticed and then volunteered that he lived nearby and came in occasionally. "I like him," she said, "and we can speak French together…but he has another girlfriend."

Well, that's good, I thought. It'd be nice to get to know this girl better without that kind of competition. Paul was in deep conversation with the girl at the end of the bar.

"How's it going?" I asked. He mumbled something, so I went back for some small conversation with Linh that wasn't really going anywhere. She seemed more interested in *Paris Match*. I asked her if she had a current boy-friend and she shook her head.

"Since my husband was killed, I have not met anyone to replace him. Maybe you?" as she smiled at me. "I joke you," she said. As I figured, but there might be something here down the road. Tho' Kim Lon from Tam Hiep was a more comfortable possibility.

Paul finally gave up on his girl, so we bid farewell with assurances that we'd be back another day and hoofed it back up Tu Do for "The Kangaroo Bar" at 5 Nguyen Thiep, the first left before the Air France office.

Paul started telling me about a girl he had met after I had left for the Army that he had decided to marry. I'm thinking that this is not at all like him. But in the end, it didn't matter because she had just written him a letter informing him of the usual…I've got a serious relationship going on, so "adios amigos." He wasn't taking it all that well.

"You know, Bill, maybe it was all in my head. It wasn't like I knew her that well, but by the time I got over here, she blossomed in my mind. She was all I could think about. Let's face it…a complete fantasy."

"Hey, I get it. Fantasies are my specialty. I'm already imagining some kind of love affair with Linh back at the bar. Considering I've hardly had any kind of affair at all, it takes some imagining. Not to mention the fantasies I've been having about Kim Lon back in Tam Hiep. Oh, fuck it. Let's stop here for another beer."

It wasn't a large place. There was a short bar at the other end with a curved stairway leading up to a second story. Maybe short time rooms. Who knows? There were half a dozen tables and chairs between the door and the bar. We grabbed a couple of empty bar stools and ordered some 33s.

"Good day, mates," said the guy sitting next to us. "I'm Sandy, Pvt. John Sanderson of the Australian Army. And you, blokes?"

We introduced ourselves and filled in with the usual Army background. Me up in the Bien Hoa/Long Binh area and Paul here in Saigon with Military Intelligence. Sandy then started right in with, "Intelligence is an oxymoron when applied to any military and certainly with you Americans. I've never seen such dumb fucks."

Paul said, "We're not that bad. All I do is look at the picture and say what's there. Great intelligence isn't required."

Sandy replied, "Well, you all must be blind as far as I can tell. None of you fuck heads know a damn thing about this war here. I came up from Malaya where we've got a similar operation going, so we Aussies know a bit about fighting these 'wogs'. We know eventually we're going to leave both colonies back with the natives. It's just sport till that happens."

I don't figure it's worth defending the "Green Machine" on this issue, or any issue really. Apparently, neither does Paul. He must still be thinking about the girl back home that's not waiting for him anymore, for he's unusually quiet. Then he piped up. "How come you're a private, Sandy, if this is your second war. You must have been in the army for a few years now."

"Fuck me, dead mate, what'd you think. I should be a staff SGT by this time, but in Singapore, I spent way too much time on Bugis Street. Was late for revile one too many mornings. What about him? I see he's a private too."

I'm starting to feel the need to defend myself. "If you want to have a life, you can't go by the Army regs all the time. I've only been busted down once and know the ropes now, so I can usually avoid a problem."

"Same here," said Sandy.

Paul was telling me about his TDY in Cu Chi where he traveled a couple of times a month. They used photo interpreters there with the 25th Infantry to fly over the countryside in a tandem two-seater, a Cessna Birddog, so he'd be able to pick out anything that looked suspicious.

"You'd think that anyone ought to be able to do that," he was saying, "but they probably figure I've got a sharper eye, considering my training and experience. Been told by some of the troops there that sometimes they bring people with my military occupational specialty (MOS) along on patrol for the same purpose. That really sounds like bullshit and I'm not looking forward to any foot pounding up in that area, especially with all the tunnels there that you hear about."

"Sounds more interesting to me," I answered. "I'm getting into a rut," thinking I'd like to get into a rut with Kim Lon back in Tam Hiep. "You know what, Paul, a couple of weeks ago, I put in a 1049 at the Orderly Room for a transfer to a long-range reconnaissance patrol (LRRP) outfit or a door gunner on a chopper but no word back yet."

"That's not how you do it," he said. "You've gotta find a spot in another outfit first, locate someone there who'll back you, and file the paperwork for that particular slot. That's what I've been told. And I'm in Military Intelligence."

I told him I'd wait a couple of more weeks to see what happens.

"Do you blokes know Tot?" asked Sandy. "She owns the place and tends bar most of the time." He introduced us to a nice-looking, middle-aged woman who spoke pretty good English. "You want more Ba Ba?" she asked. That's Thirty-Three beer for the uninformed, a leftover from the French who probably still own the brewery for that matter. She poured us all a round.

"Hey, Sandy, who's the girl at the end of the bar?" He turned toward her saying "Kanh, come down here. These blokes need to meet a real Saigon woman."

She walked over to us; she was a bit sassy and introduced herself. Being a real knockout and knowing it, she made no move to force herself like maybe saying "You buy me tea," though her presence in the bar meant that. Ordinarily, the girls weren't paid any salary and had to split their drink money, usually coke, fifty–fifty with the owners.

"You want a tea?" asked Paul.

"You no from Australia," she answered.

"You're damn right," he shot back, "I'm from New York."

"You wanna remember this is an Aussie bar," said Sandy, with a hint of a smile. "Keep that New York shit to yourself."

"North Country," said Paul. "We live 300 miles north of NYC, in fact just an hour south of Montreal." Sandy found that agreeable saying that he lived in the bush in Australia, miles from any city.

A tall, good-looking guy in jungle fatigues came in and pulled up a stool beside Sandy. Paul was engaged in conversation with Kanh.

"Good day, mate," said Sandy. "Haven't seen you around lately."

"I've been out with the diggers in Bia Ria for an operation. Got some great photos for *Paris Match*."

"You know these blokes here?" asked Sandy.

Getting a negative response, he introduced us. It turned out that it was the photographer Sean Flynn that I'd just been talking about with Linh, the bar girl down the street.

"Just met a friend of yours down at the Gala Bar," I said. "A girl named Linh who just happened to be reading *Paris Match* that had some of your photos published."

"That's good to hear. Linh's a great girl and quite beautiful, as you now know. We have great conversations in French. So where are you guys stationed? I'm about to take a run to Lai Khe for an operation with the Big Red One."

Paul answered, "I'm with the 4th MI Battalion over at Tan Son Nhut. Bill here is in Long Binh. What's going on in Lai Khe?"

"I'm not sure," said Flynn, but the word with the Aussies in Vung Tau is that something big had happened but was being kept in the QT. Thought it'd be interesting to check out. Haven't been up that way yet."

Neither of us had either, but Paul started filling him in on Cu Chi, which caught his attention. Sandy started talking about some Aussie operations in the Bien Hoa area that they carry out with the 173rd Airborne that's headquartered at the air base there. He was in Bia Ria near Vung Tau most of the time running patrols in that area. The only highway between Saigon and Vung Tau runs right by our compound. I've been tempted to make a run there. Supposedly, great sandy beaches with an army R&R compound available.

In the French time here, that area was called Cap St. Jacques. During the hot months, which seemed to me to be most of the year, all the in crowd from Saigon spent as much time as they could in this resort. It was not possible to drive an army vehicle on that highway between Bien Hoa and Vung Tau these days without being in a convoy. The VC might get you along the way, or the MPs might pick you up at either end.

"Hey, good meeting both of you guys, but we gotta get going. I need to get back to Long Binh before dark and don't care to get lost. It's been a great day so far. Maybe see you blokes again sometime."

"Stop in here when you're in town," said Sandy. "This is the most interesting joint in all of Saigon. Just ask Tot…or Khanh. Hope to see you fellas again."

"Linh says the Gala is," said Flynn, "but this is the meeting place to be in the know about what's going on with the GIs and the news people. It's common knowledge that the hot shots prefer the rooftop bar at the Carvelle for the most recent updates; however, the old 'Kangaroo' is a good second. A little like 'Givral' the coffee shop on the corner across from the Continental that's 'headquarters' for the government politicians. See you boys again someday maybe."

After saying our farewells to them and the girls, Paul and I hiked across the square to the Continental to hire a cyclo back to his compound.

"If we have time, let's have one more drink at the company club. I want to show you the girl there that lets me screw her if I get a room. She's great and I don't have to pay. Maybe some of the boys will be there too."

Paul always was being a cheap bastard, so this was expected. "What does she let you do?" I asked.

"Anything kinky."

"Well, actually she likes a little tongue in the old bung, if you know what I mean. That's right up my alley anyway, you know that…and as you might expect, it's part of the deal."

"Leave me the hell out of all that," I said. "When are you going back up to Cu Chi?"

"Who knows? They don't give me much warning. I'd just as soon hang around here for a while. Let's get back. You'll want to reach Long Binh before dark."

After catching another cyclo back to 69 Dong Da, it was up to their club for one more. Paul's girl Hanh was there, and she was all that he said, quiet but sexy. Apparently, the rest of the company was working or sleeping for we were alone.

Hitching a ride north seemed simple enough, though I wasn't all that sure of the way. Getting to the Newport Bridge on the drive in was straightforward; however, I hadn't paid that much attention after crossing. As it turned out, another bridge came into view, a steel-framed contraption that sufficed for all traffic including trains. It was too narrow for a deuce-and-a-half; however, a five-quarter or jeep would likely make it.

After a half hour or so, I was back in the countryside. This area wasn't moist like rice fields and almost reminded me of cow pastures back home. Then I noticed a column of troops crossing the road up ahead. A couple of choppers were circling off in the distance to the East. It was not clear from this angle what was going on. One lobbed off a pod of rockets, and the troops began double timing in that direction.

I began to get a little nervous since I was not only AWOL, I didn't know where I was, and I certainly was not equipped for a firefight if that's what was going to be happening. As I got closer, a voice called out to me in English.

"Hey, where you go?" It was a soldier in a uniform that vaguely resembled US fatigues.

"I'm trying to get back to Long Binh but am having a little trouble. What's going on?"

"Not sure, maybe some VC in the field. Look like maybe helicopter shoot them. Gunfire all finished. My name Omar."

I'm thinking then, Omar, what the fuck? "What kind of name is that for a Vietnam GI?"

"You know, like Omar Sharif…Lawrence of Arabia. American GI say that I look like him so now that my name." This is a new one for me.

"I am an interpreter for the 199th Light Infantry Brigade," said Omar. "Went to see friend this morning and ended up here. We have some beer tonight then I go home to my unit. They in Long Binh."

Now I was getting somewhere. "How do I get to Long Binh?"

"Couple mile ahead take road to Thu Duc. It go straight to highway."

After some more small talk, Omar left as he had to catch up with the unit. He did say that he had a girlfriend in Tam Hiep and that maybe we'd meet again. It'd be great to have someone who knew both worlds and could speak good English.

A little later, a Lambretta came along with half a dozen people in the back, but they made room for me to Thu Duc, and from there, I walked to the highway and quickly hitched a ride in a jeep the few miles back to the main gate. It felt good. Great trip to Saigon, hooked up with Paul, met a beauty plus a couple of interesting bars to stop in next time in town…plus Sandy and Flynn. A great day overall.

Dusk was settling in, but it was too early for me to stop at the company club. The path to Tam Hiep looked rather enticing, so I took a walk in that direction to see if Kim Lon was home. The traffic was light, a reminder that New Year's day was still in effect. A couple of kids were alone on the path as I trailed along into the village. The girl tending the coffee stand at the so-called village square, more like a wide spot where three alleys converged, told me that Kim Lon had gone up to Ho Nai with a friend. It looked like it'd be another day before I'd get anywhere with her.

CHAPTER 3

I woke up suddenly realizing that a mosquito net was staring me in the face. Such a downer for in the dream minutes past, the beautiful Linh from the bar in Saigon was tight beside me. The dream of a rather vigorous coupling among other delicious sexual tidbits was already fading, and a whistle could be heard. Damn, the vision is gone, and SGT Judd will be calling for an early morning formation.

"Hey, Santimaw, get your ass up. There're a lot of guys that are going to need covering this morning." There is a slight, barely distinguishable mumble out of him, as I'd expect. Larry stayed up every night late smoking and drinking and bullshitting. There was hardly a story of the farm country outside of Sacramento and the Mexican girls that populated it and got porked on a regular basis, that I hadn't heard more than once. However, that never stopped him no matter the lateness of the evening.

Eventually, most of the hooch was dressing as the whistle blew for formation and some sort of configuration filled the dirt area in front of the tents. SGT Judd was walking back and forth, mumbling, in front of the men as he moved. He had been retired for a few years but was called up for this "sorry excuse" of a war. And he never let us forget how sorry it was and we were. After all, most of the old sergeants like him had been in the big one, the Second World War, the real war. The last real war. And furthermore, they didn't appreciate being pulled out of retirement for this last hurrah. Certainly, SGT Judd didn't. He much preferred fishing for catfish near his home somewhere in the deep south.

He started calling our roll call by squad.

"Easey, La Rosa, Santimaw, Romano, etc.," and for each, there was some sort of reply. More like mumbling, for half of the company was only there in spirit. Some didn't crawl out of bed. Some spent the night in Tam Hiep or Bien Hoa and were late getting back through the wire. That could always be a problem. If some prick pulled guard on the main gate, there could be some difficulty. None of us looked like VC, but who knows the thinking?

SGT Judd noticed that the formation was a little weak but didn't make any accusations. Just this.

"I know you men are down there in these towns chasing the women. Most of them ain't big enough to take a dick, and half of you are down there eatin' it. This has to stop. The captain is going to catch on, and we're all going to be fucked. So let's get with it, all of you, and tell your asshole friends, the ghost soldiers, what I said." Most of the men mocked SGT Judd, but in his own way, he was looking out for them.

With that I headed for the mess hall for coffee and eggs. Most of these guys bitched, but I loved army food. Coffee, fresh eggs much of the time, toast, shit on a shingle all the time, sometimes potatoes…dehydrated, but so what. Juice. Bacon too. How could you beat it? They were pumping out the food by six and stayed open till after eight, especially since the Ammo Dump blew, for the night patrols, listening posts, and ambush sites weren't back in the company area till then. Any luck and I'd be back on tonight and have a few days off.

There had been some incoming mortars down past the motor pool late last night. SGT Judd sent half a dozen of us down to fill sand bags to refortify the trenches along the wire in that area. Some of the guard posts were also lacking, even though the view into the country side on the southern end of Long Binh was pleasant enough, but perhaps not for the grunts that were "humping the boonies" as they say, in that area.

As luck would have it, several girls from the local villages were filling sand bags as we neared the trench system. There was one beauty and I hoped she's working here today. Sometimes, just the presence of a beautiful girl is more than enough. It's so simple, just look and smile and be glad you're alive.

She was…and I found out from the GI running the crew that her name was Hanh. I edged over toward her as the bagging progressed.

"How are you, Hanh?" She looked my way and said nothing. "You speak English?" and she nodded silently.

"Can you talk?" I asked.

"No can do," she answered. "I no trust GI no more."

Fair enough. I'd keep her in view while shoveling sand. While tying off the bag, I noticed the guy next to me was using a miller's knot. He's gotta be off the farm someplace.

"Where'd you learn to tie that knot?" I asked.

"Riding a combine. The old man and I farm it in the country south of Cleveland. My name's Joe Easly, How about you?"

"Bill Collins…same background but up in northern New York. What kind of combine you guys use?"

It turned out he was ahead of us. We were still using a McCormick-Deering from the thirties. His people had moved up to a 1958 self-propelled Massey–Harrris, which would have caused great envy on our farm. We talked about cows, crops, horses, etc., for a spell and somehow got into girls. Joe here hadn't been involved with any of the locals. Like most of the regular troops, he stuck pretty close to home. Maybe went down to Bien Hoa on payday for some drinks but that was about it. A lot of them wrote letters at night looking at a picture of their girlfriend or wife. I preferred looking and touching the real thing. He was ahead of me back in the world though.

"You know what I liked best back on the farm?" he asked. "No," I wondered, "what is it?"

"I like a warm rainy day in the summer when you can't bale hay because of a light rain that's begun. We've got a couple of teenage girls, our cousins actually, who help us out in the mow. Once or twice, one of them, Cindy's her name, let me screw her in the hay when we ended up there alone. It seemed like we were both lagging behind. Oh, man, there was nothing like it. Just screwing away with the rain beating on a tin roof keeping up with the rhythm of the rain drops. Absolutely nothing like it."

I think he had a point, never being that lucky myself. But I knew a Cindy back home who came to visit in the summer. Who knows, maybe when I get back…In the meantime, back to filling sand bags and reinforcing the tops of the trenches. It looked as if the bunker on the corner had been damaged. That might give us another day of this. Pretty good duty with the girls working here and all.

In the background to this detail, we could hear some light explosions a little to the south. Just then an F-100 Super Sabre flew over low, diving in on that same spot, letting loose a couple cannisters of Napalm. The flames blew up like hell. Then, an F-4 Phantom flew a repeat.

"You see that, Easly. I wonder what the hell's going on."

Two Huey Gunships showed up and dove down letting go pods of rockets. This kind of assault went on for at least an hour; fighters blended in with the choppers, a great show. There didn't appear to be any native houses, and it wasn't apparent that any GIs had been inserted. Must have been some kind of intel indicating a VC presence. Maybe photo interpreting from Paul's 4th Military Intelligence Battalion. We were perched on a knoll with a great view that overlooked the battle site.

It was apparent that the girls were becoming agitated. Who knew? They might have friends or relatives on the receiving end of this explosive power. The Dong Nai Regiment, known by the locals as the 274th VC Main Force Regiment, was staffed by locals and had been since early in the French War. The Dong Nai River formed the southern border of Long Binh Post.

Two more Huey gunships flew over at a low altitude with mini guns blazing. Still nothing was apparent near the site they were firing on. Finally, a fleet of choppers could be heard in the distance. As they approached in a trail formation, at a much higher altitude than the gunships, it became apparent that they were slicks, possibly loaded with troops to be inserted below our position. Easly and I were looking up when suddenly it appeared that pieces of junk started falling. Instantly, it was apparent that two Hueys were falling, possibly from a midair, as pieces of the blades of both machines were falling separately. GIs were then seen falling from the fuselages, arms and legs waving, with no possibility of survival.

"How the fuck did that happen?" asked Easly as the machines, the blades, and the bodies slammed into the ground a few hundred yards below us. The site immediately burst into flames. No possibility of rescue, of any kind. Another Huey landed near the inferno.

It didn't appear to be from the original flight. Very shortly, a Dust Off showed up. We were only a couple of miles from the 93rd Evacuation Hospital; however, nothing and nobody could help these poor guys. We and the girls were visibly shaken. Hanh, the beautiful one, had tears in her eyes. It was quiet for some time. But as always, especially here, life goes on.

Later in the day, two other guys from the company were working down the line from us, back bagging after settling in since the choppers fell. Washington, a Black from Georgia and Cobbs a Kentucky redneck. Oddly enough, they were friends, after a fashion. Washington had faced a court martial back at Ft. Gordon before this station. Murder charges stemming from a knife fight with a working girl in downtown Augusta, Georgia. He swore self-defense, and it stuck. Cobb had spent a few years in Germany earlier. His uncle was a general in this man's army. His grandfather had been the first convict executed in the Ohio electric chair, for murder. We had all kinds in this Company of regulars.

Cobbs yelled for some water, so I sent down my canteen. He shared it with Washington who then handed it over to Hanh. It was a very hot day. As Cobbs saw her beginning to drink, he yelled "What the hell are you doing. You gooks can't drink water from our canteen." The poor girl didn't know the next move. Washington blew up.

"Cobbs, what the fuck are you saying to that girl. She's thirsty, just as thirsty as us."

"Well, she ain't us, she's a gook," said Cobbs. He wouldn't let up. Washington looked like he was going to blow.

"Can't you guys drop it," I said. "It's my canteen, and I'd love to place my tongue on hers, so I sure as hell don't give a damn if she drinks from it."

"From what I've heard of you, Cobbs, with the short time girls in Bien Hoa, a little saliva on the water jug is nothing to the mix of female fluids that you're accustomed too."

"It ain't the same thing," he answered. "But fuck it, forget about it."

It's too bad. There are at least twenty GIs dead from that chopper crash that we all just witnessed, and we've got to have that kind of disagreement over who can drink the water. I know Washington is extremely touchy when it comes to race. It was good to see him come to the girl's defense. Be nice to think that Cobbs learned a thing or two, but my experience with the boys from the South is that the racism was so saturated that this generation was never going to shed it. Too bad. The serious issue was that those twenty GIs who were at this moment, being "bagged and tagged" were never going to have a life.

I wandered off early from sand bagging detail, lost in thought about those poor souls that just bought the farm. You could usually slip out by five maybe a little earlier on most details…or permanent jobs…which sometimes gave the possibility of more freedom. There was always the chance that Kim Lon hadn't left for Tam Hiep, though it was getting late in the day. She washed a mountain of GI laundry most evenings.

I can't get the sight of those guys backpedaling down to the ground out of my head as I passed the motor pool. What a way to go. The five-ton dump was parked near the shop, so it must have been "rescued" permanently from the unit in Xuan Loc that loaned it to the company. It occurred to me that if we had to use it in the morning before sand bagging, it would be possible to truck up a few loads from the point along the Dong Nai River where some military contractor was sucking sand from the river middle, probably for mixing concrete. It would bag a great deal easier than the rough stuff we were using here.

It was quiet down at the motor pool. They must have all split too. Hell, why not. The word is that things will be picking up very soon. Some big operation over in the Iron Triangle that's spear headed by the 1st Infantry Division, the legendary Big Red One, up in Di An, a few miles SW of the highway intersection with the river. We provided support for most of the outfits operating in this area. Bertzik drove the ten-ton wrecker from salvage, many times late at night. It wasn't unusual to find trucks, APCs, and occasionally tanks loaded and parked in the Company street in the morning, that had been blown up to hell, sometimes burned to hell. The radio shop was constantly supplied with prick twenty-fives (PRC-25), the common infantry backpack two-way radios that were full of bullet holes. The radio man being the first in the company the VC shot, as he called in the air strikes.

Three Dust Offs were settling in on the landing pads alongside of the 93rd Evacuation Hospital as I neared their area. More poor bastards being flown in to be patched up…or bagged up. Quite an operation here. I'd submitted a 10-49 requesting a transfer to the chopper unit that was stationed at the hospital area. I never heard back on that request. Probably thrown in the basket along with all the others, while admitting that I had no idea how to arrange a transfer.

The road was dusty. The 93rd Evac choppers were stirring up a dust storm even tho' the pads in the hospital compound were blacktop. I could see Santimaw and Banks up ahead hoofing it toward the club it looked like. Our Company had its own, homemade out of scrap lumber, but it worked. For some reason, liquor wasn't sold, just beer, soda, and slot machines. Ten cents would buy anything in the house. And then there was the juke box. The problem being there was the ongoing jukebox battle between the soul brothers and the rednecks. Whoever got there first would pack it with their songs, which occasionally erupted into a difficult situation. But hopefully not tonight. And thinking about it further, you had to worry about more than the songs. A couple of nights ago, one of the drunks got pissed off, went back to his hooch, and came back in with his M-14 locked and loaded. Luckily, he was jumped and disarmed before someone was shot.

And then I saw Kim walking along with that shoulder stick beside her neck, loaded up with two huge laundry bags.

"Hey, Kim, wait up a minute. I need to talk with you."

She turned and smiled. That was a good start.

"No have time for talk," she said. "I have work. It very heavy."

I offered to carry it for her to the house in Tam Hiep, but she declined. I don't think she wanted the neighbors thinking she was involved this early in the day.

"How about if I stop over after dark to see you. Maybe we can have a coke at the stand in the square."

She wasn't that keen on a visit, but I offered to carry her load of laundry down to the village edge. It was so heavy. I was amazed that she was able to lift it up let alone walk any distance. Walking along behind her allowed me a great view of her behind. These black pajama peasant garb items of clothing lacked the effect of form fitting jeans; however, with a little imagination, they fit well enough. She was getting more desirable by the step. However, soon it was back to the main gate.

The odds were that Banks and Santimaw were at the club for an extended period so after dropping in at the mess hall for some solid nourishment, I hoofed it over. This home-made shack, and it really looked like one, had become a home away from home for most of the troops living in the company area, as well as anyone passing by or passing through from units in the countryside. On occasion, entertainment was provided; sometimes, girl bands from the states. Word was that "The Three Kittens" were scheduled for later in the month, and we had had the country western singer Hank Snow preform for Christmas time. No Bob Hope for us. And "The Three Kittens" weren't actually famous anywhere but the GI beer halls in Vietnam. As far as I knew, they were formed for that very purpose.

Soul brother music was playing as I entered. Banks and Santimaw were sitting at the bar. There was no obvious Black or redneck presence.

"So, you getting anywhere with the Cambodia girl?" asked Banks. "I told you to just do it like we do in Arkansas, just ask her if she wants to fuck."

"No way; I can do that," I answered. "I don't really know how to. I'm thinking it can lead to that in a bit if I stick to it."

"You mean if you keep leering at her, silently, while carrying her load. I saw you walk off in the direction of Tam Hiep while we were heading this way."

"That's how we do it in the fields south of Sacramento too," volunteered Santimaw.

He had spoken many times of his sexual escapades while working with the Mexicans in that area where he lived before joining the army. He liked baling hay especially. The Mexican girls helped load, and he'd get them on the wagon tops while riding into the barns. I knew the same scene back home but had never got a girl on the wagon top, great idea that it was.

"Those girls were so hot," he drooled while remembering. "But I gotta admit I love these girls here just as much. This is a great place. You gotta get with it, Collins, if you want a girlfriend. Otherwise, it'll be short time houses and car washes for you till you rotate."

I was ready to change the topic. "What's going on with the Ammo Dump? Any word about us going back on that detail? I'm ready to get the hell out of this company area anytime."

"I think tomorrow night," said Santimaw.

That'd be great I was thinking. It was time to move on from sand bagging.

CHAPTER 4

THE sun was settling as we rode out of the company in the back of a small fleet of deuce-and-a-halfs. The civilian workers for RMK BRJ were walking down the highway heading home. As always, a few clowns threw c-ration cans at some of them. Target practice they said, but a can of bread or ham and lima beans could hurt like hell if you got clipped on the back of the head or between the shoulder blades. No matter what you said, they wouldn't stop. It was the GI verses the Gook thing. Let's face it, most of these guys had in no way gone "Native" as they used to say in the British Empire. They didn't mind screwing the short time girls, but it went no farther than that for most of them. The vilification of the Vietnamese people by the American military was alive and well.

The Americans were like the English. Going "native" wasn't approved of. It wasn't quite proper. This was one of the great differences in methods of colonialism. The French in Indo China went "native" all the time from the looks of a good number of younger people here. In fact, it looked as if they had been busier than hell going "native."

I missed not seeing and talking with Kim the next day. They'd put me on a detail driving ammo from the docks in Cogido on the Dong Nai River to the ammo depot, which was a good job. You drove army Five Tons with forty-feet flatbeds loaded with pallets of all kinds of ammunition from barges in the docks to the staging area not so far from our company area. And I mean all kinds of ammunition: aircraft machine gun ammo, rockets, bombs, artillery shells, napalm, just about anything you could think of. The Long Binh Ammo Depot, aka ammo dump, was known to be the largest of its kind in the world. Later that night, we would all be on ammo dump detail.

Santimaw, Banks, and Washington were along in the same truck. Any luck we would be able to set up on the same ambush site or listening post, whatever kind of job they gave us. Then we could cover each other, keep just one of us up at a time rather than half of the squad as was the standard operating procedure. We drove at least a couple of miles till reaching the staging area where the troops were organized into small squads for the night's mission.

As luck would have it, the four of us were picked for one ambush site. We loaded back in a truck and were driven down to the far corner on the NE of the pads where only one row of concertina wire separated the ammo depot from the jungle that extended to Xuan Loc, a few miles farther east.

As was the custom, after being positioned by the SGT of the guard, we moved some distance away for two reasons. We didn't want to be caught sleeping on guard, tho' we always kept one man awake, and we didn't want our location to be known by any VC who might be watching from the bush. Obviously, we made the move after dark.

"Oh, man," said Santimaw. "I don't feel like digging any foxhole tonight. Fuck it."

None of us did. There was a sag behind some brush where we set up that looked to be safe enough. After stretching out our bedrolls, Washington set out a couple of claymores and took the first watch. Looked like a peaceful night.

Banks and Santimaw lit up a joint, carefully shielded, and began talking about pussy once more; their favorite topic.

"You know," said Banks. "I haven't had a snapping pussy since my wife in Thailand."

"What the fuck!" said Santimaw. "You've never talked of a wife before. What the hell's that all about?"

"Well, I ain't too proud of it," said Banks. "I kind of ran out on her when I left Thailand. Had a couple of kids too."

"Banks," I said. "I never thought you were that fucking low."

"It's not like that," said Banks. "I got in some trouble in Bangkok, like selling army property. The First SGT liked me; he got me shipped out overnight somehow.

I couldn't get back there in any reasonable way without getting locked up, and after a while, you know how it goes, I lost interest. Now I'm stuck over here."

"Sounds pretty fucking weak to me," I said. "But who's to judge?"

"What about the snapping pussy?" said Santimaw. "That's my interest."

"Do you guys read books?" I asked. "There are other topics of interest in this world, like tonight, for instance. What if Charlie starts shooting at us?" Then I remembered that we had moved position after darkness set in. We should be safe enough, and we were.

Washington came in on schedule and woke me up, and then by the time the others did their shift, dawn began breaking. When we eventually made it back to the mess hall, the egg man had left, so we settled for coffee and shit on the shingle. It tasted great I thought. The others bitched like hell but cleaned it all up. I fell asleep back in the hooch dreaming about Kim Lon. Dreaming about Cambodia, the "Gentle Land" of old French legends.

A few nights later we were back at it. A listening post rather nearby the location of our last ambush site. This time no Washington. His spot was taken by a PFC Wilton from the 25th Infantry down from Cu Chi. There were times the slots out here in the Dump couldn't be filled by locals from Long Binh, and troops were brought in from the "boonies." Hence, Wilton. We considered the Cu Chi area, "the boonies." Anything outside the wire was hostile territory. Underground in the Division area was hostile territory. Tunnels everywhere. Santimaw took the first shift. The rest of us back of the berm started talking.

"You're not a Tunnel Rat, are you, Wilton?" I asked after Banks had slipped off snoring away.

"Do I fucking look like it? I'm six feet tall and weigh one hundred sixty pounds. Only a little shit can do that job. You see the size of most of these gooks. They can double time through those tunnels on their knees. They pop up outside the wire most every day and pick off one of our guys. I hate the fuckers. I can't for the life of me see how you guys go downtown and fuck 'em. I'd shoot every goddam one of them if it was up to me."

That was quite a mouthful. I noticed that a lot of guys from the field were like that. They didn't really know any civilians on a personal level; he sure as hell wasn't interested in them; period. I figured to try and change the subject.

"I can understand the VC grunts, but the girls downtown are another matter. They're just trying to survive like everyone over here. Cut 'em some slack and enjoy yourself. What the fuck."

"I don't give a goddamn what you guys do. I hate the fuckers. You have 'em kill enough of your friends, and you'll feel the same."

Guess I should try and really change the subject.

"You been in any hard ass firefights lately, Wilton?" I asked.

"Yea, I have. With those fucking gooks…almost eighteen hours. I lost three friends, and more than a dozen were wounded. It started out we were midway, more or less, between Cu Chi and the Cambodia border. It had been a nice day and a slow patrol. Didn't seem to be no rush, no contact, and we had been dug in for the night. Quiet way past midnight. Then around two or three o'clock, all hell broke loose. It was so damn dark that it was difficult to get organized. We never really did. Too much goddam fire. You know how they are. Usually hit hard and fast, then draw back and disappear before Air can be called in."

While he kept on talking, I was thinking that we here had been damn lucky so far. An occasional sniper and maybe a quick skirmish. The only recent causality had been Sparks who had been shot in the face by his own man. What a fuck up that was. But Wilton wasn't finished.

"So damn dark, we called in for chopper support but no way to direct them where to fire. The gooks were too close, and it was pitch dark. No moon. Fuck me. The squads were spread out over an area that wasn't clearly known to each of us. Tracers going everywhere. Screaming down the line. No way to know who it was or how to help them. Our medic was busy with our squad, which eventually lost two and had over half wounded. This shit went on all day. We couldn't really figure out where they were. Anyhow, by the end of the day, we were all shot up to hell."

I told him I was sorry about his friends, and about how lucky we had been. He grew quiet, lost in thought. Didn't say any more about that incident. About then, Santimaw turned up looking pretty tired, and Wilton took over the guard position. I rolled over and started dreaming about Kim Lon and then must have nodded off to sleep.

When Wilton's shift was up, he woke up both Banks and me. It was Bobby D's turn who grumbled, sleepily, as he more or less crawled to the guard post. It was still dark as hell. Wilton wasn't sleepy and seemed like he wanted to continue the conversation. I, who loved the idea of flying but had never been a pilot, began asking him about any helicopter inserts or other chopper operations that he might have been on.

"Yea, there was one," said Wilton. "You wouldn't believe it, but a hundred Huey's and the target were across the line in Cambodia, or so they told us."

Me, I'd believe anything about the US military at this point. It never looked to me like the rules applied, so I wasn't skeptical about his telling.

"I don't think we were in the air half an hour. You know where Cu Chi is. Not that far from the 'Parrots Beak,' the piece of Cambodia that veers into VN pointing toward Saigon. Anyhow, settling in territory that looked just like home in VN, we at first found nothing. Not a soul or a building. So, we started hoofing through the brush and eventually came on a settlement. Now you gotta remember, we'd lost a lot of good men recently, and there was no good opinion of the locals. The gooks. Fuck man, we opened up and eventually killed every living thing, even the dogs and the chickens. A bad scene but what can you do. I don't know anymore."

I didn't know either, what I was thinking, but was glad not to have been there. Wilton grew quiet again and eventually went off to his bed roll. I sat up thinking till Banks came in, and by the time my watch ended, dawn was breaking in the East. We came upon a memorable scene while loaded in the deuce-and-a-half waiting for the drive in. A five quarter came by, windshield down, covered with sandbags and red dust with two large German Shepherds draped over the front fenders. The four or five troopers in the vehicle were also covered with red dust, almost a view out of the French Foreign Legion.

Someone had a radio playing and at six in the morning, every day began with "Gooooood Morning, Vietnam," followed by the Rolling Stones this wonderful morning. If only my camera had been along. I'd taken a few good shots of Kim and kept it with me often. A Miranda from the PX. I had fantasies of doing like Flynn from the "Kangaroo" in Saigon whenever I took leave of this army. It looked as if the war would be going on forever or close to it.

And as it happened, we weren't guys in the field who had to mount up about this time in the morning and put in another day humping the boonies. We were REMFs and had the day off. With a good breakfast of bacon and eggs packed into my stomach and at loose ends, I figured I'd look up Kim and see where she was at. See if she was "thinking about me." It turned out she was sunning herself down along the main row of tents and home-made hooches.

"Kim, how are you today?" She looked my way and smiled.

"My friend you," she answered, "I am good. Where you go yesterday? I look but I no find you."

This was interesting. She was actually looking for me.

"I go with friends. To the club. Drink beer. If I know that you wanted to see me, I never go with them. I go with you." Not that I agreed with speaking this kind of broken English with the local girls, but it was simpler. Fewer explanations.

"Oh you like drink beer with your friends, not spend time with Kim."

"Never happen." was my reply. The sight of her infectious smile beat drinking any amount of beer with Santimaw and Banks. No doubt about that.

"I was thinking that maybe tonight I could go to Tam Hiep and see you. Maybe have soda together at the village stand."

"Not tonight," she said. "But later we can do."

A day later, we did. A miracle happened.

A few beers with the boys at the club was more than enough. It was after eight, pretty dark, so I walked down to the main gate and as luck would have it Bertizik was on.

"Hey, Bertizik, Bill Collins. How's the guard set up for tonight?"

"Good, real good. Where the fuck you heading? Tam Hiep?"

"Yea, I might be late so didn't want a problem getting back in."

"No sweat, GI, Washington and then Cobbs. You're good till after midnight."

I thanked him, and then got to talking and asked if he'd been out at night for any interesting missions lately. He had.

"A track unit from the 11th Armored Cav. got hit hard just off Highway 1 a couple of klicks this side of Xuan Loc. Burned the shit out of two of 'em. I don't know how many got out before it burned, but it didn't look good. The fucking thing was full of bullet holes too. I loaded up the two APCs and trucked 'em back here to the motor pool. It didn't like there was much in the way of salvage I'll tell you. Just scrap iron. You know we're lucky as shit down here."

"You don't have to tell me." I said. "You wouldn't think a couple of miles could make that much difference."

"Well, you know," said Bertzik "It ain't all that safe here, really. Couple of days ago, I had to pick up a K P deuce-and-a-half between Ho Nai and Bien Hoa that had been shot up and burned. I don't think anyone was hurt, just wanted to scare 'em. Hell, the girls get too much free food off the drivers. They feed half the VC families in the area."

"Whadda you think, Collins, they all VC?"

"Could be," I said. "Could be…but who cares?"

"Two months to go," said Bertzik "and my ass is out of here…hopefully in one piece."

That seemed to be the frame of mind of most of the troops that I talked with. There was always that contingent of "John Wayne" types, holdovers from the mindset of fathers and uncles that had been in the Second World War, the big one, who were what I guess you could call patriots, whatever the hell that was, who could be found up in the club. They went to town once a month on pay days and otherwise stayed inside the wire. Most of these REMFs never got their ass near real trouble. I left Bertzik and headed down the trail to Tam Hiep.

A crowd of kids had congregated at the village stand. A black GI sat in the center of them in striped pajamas having a coke. The kids were all eating snails. I could find no sign of Kim. The truth was the short time girl gig was getting old. I needed a girlfriend. Not really needed one but wanted one, but not like a wife. And probably not like Miss Mai from the East Hotel who was a good friend.

Never having been to Paris, I wouldn't know, but Mai was what I thought a French whore would be like. She even had a bidet in her room not to mention her performance. I'd never seen a bidet before, but it was the line at her door during pay day that led me to believe that she wouldn't make a very personal girlfriend. I figured Kim could make one; however, I never forgot my time with Miss Mai.

I'd been walking around Bien Hoa alone after a night on a listening post and stopped in at the East Hotel thinking maybe a little blackjack with the girls. Mai was alone.

She said "Collins, why you no come to my bed with me?"

Being a little bashful around her, I couldn't explain why. I said that it was near the end of the month, and I was short of money.

"I no care," she said, "You pay me other time."

So, I took her up on it, entered her room with the bidet, and stripped off my clothes. And so did she, which displayed a delicious body, somewhat fuller than what was considered normal here. So far, she certainly didn't look normal.

She began by nuzzling around my face and neck and then my stomach with her hands around my you know what that stiffened enormously, and that's not kidding. And then there was more, and it all went on for some time. Already far longer than a normal short time for a person with my background who didn't have much to compare it to. I didn't have anything to compare it to; period.

After getting with the program, I told Mai "I think I love you." She shot right back after freeing up her lips, so to speak, with "Don't bull shit me, GI. We just pretend to make love. It not for real."

I was thinking OK, let's keep pretending, and after a little more licking on both our parts, that's what we did. Pretend like hell till we got right to the missionary and prayed like hell till things exploded. By the time I came around, Mai was using the bidet which I'd never seen either. All in all an interesting and informative and very pleasurable afternoon.

Back to reality here in Tam Hiep, I ordered a beer with ice. Almost every joint sold 33, the standard French product for I don't know how many years in Indo China. The first of the Bs of the 3 Bs of French Colonialism, the other two being Bistros and Bordellos. The French were on the right track but ultimately fucked it all up.

"Hey, man, what's your name?" It was the GI in the pajamas.

"Collins" I said. "Isn't it a little early for bedtime?" He smiled and said that he was escaping the world, relaxing before bedtime. Funny I hadn't run into him before if he was the Tam Hiep regular he seemed to be. The kids were all laughing and kidding around while they all begged me for some money. I was just hoping that Kim would show up. She liked tea, and it was tea time most any time in Vietnam. And then I saw her walking up the path from her place, a tiny little house near the frog ponds where the village boys could be found during the sunny days. She took a seat beside me and ordered a tea...not a Saigon Tea.

"You look for me, Collin," she stated matter of factly. "My friend you."

"You know I always look for you, Kim Lon. You are my dream."

"Oh no, have many girlfriends you," she replied.

This was leading into the standard conversation between a local girl and a GI, so somehow, I had to change the subject.

"Were you able to finish your laundry work?" I asked. "Looked like a big load."

"I fini long time," she said. "You want to come to my house for tee tee chop chop?"

That was the invitation I'd been waiting for...for a long time. I wasn't interested in the little bit of food. Maybe the other kind of Chop Chop. We walked hand in hand down the path to her house which by itself meant little. They all walked hand in hand, the girls, the boys, and sometimes the girls and the boys. This was a one-room house, a warm weather one-room house, but all you would ever need. There was a big bed against the wall.

We sat down on a bench by the table. She didn't bother with the little bit of food, so I inched closer and she didn't move away. Kim had always been a friendly girl.

I tried to kiss her. And she responded in kind. Not a wet kiss but a real kiss, which was unusual for the Vietnamese. They were more into rubbing noses on your cheek or maybe the edge of your nose. Perhaps it was the dark blood from Cambodia. A couple of more little kisses and I edged my hand under her armpit toward her small but very firm breasts. She didn't push my hand away. She edged herself closer, almost tucked into my side. My God, I touched her little nipples and nearly swooned myself for I hadn't had much experience, even with white girls. I never knew what to say to them. Consequently, our conversations were always a bit strained. Over here it was less complicated…much less complicated.

"Maybe Kim we can lie down in your bed and make love."

"For sure," she said, "but we no can make love. Have blood. Maybe in three days."

For me that was better. It took the pressure off. We did move to her bed and snuggled for a long time. Only a little feeling up before both of us drifted off to sleep. I awakened much later and figured I'd better get going, not having any idea who was guarding the main gate. I didn't wake Kim, just kissed her on the cheek and continued breathing in her scent.

CHAPTER 5

SGT Judd was holding morning formation, and it wasn't going well. There weren't enough troops to even fake it. I was pretty damn tired. The guy at the gate wouldn't let me in so I had to crawl underneath the concertina wire in back of the PX that was on the knoll overlooking Tam Hiep. That wasn't too sensible because there were guard duty guys on the perimeter fencing all night. Luckily, it was late enough that they must have been drowsy.

"Where the hell are they?" he yelled. "Are these worthless fuckheads still sleeping or are they all in Bien Hoa trying to stick a dick in those little girls down there. Don't they know we're supposed to fighting a god damned war here. Don't any of 'em have a fucking brain in their heads?"

"I'll tell you one thing, we didn't have this problem in the big one, the Second World War, or Korea either. We had real men fighting those wars, not fucking punks like you people. Get the fuck up and make this formation he yelled," this time loud enough to provoke a response.

Enough guys must have awakened with his yelling and were slipping out the back of the hooch filling out the squads enough to pass muster, for SGT Judd dismissed the company without even taking roll call. A good start for the morning thus far. Banks and Santimaw happened to be in the formation, so we walked down to the mess hall together.

"So, Collins, you getting anywhere with that black hooch girl?" asked Banks.

I'm not interested in discussing my potential relationship with Kim Lon with any of these GIs. I know where the conversation will go. The usual gook bullshit about how they are all whores, thieves, etc., though Banks and Santimaw had some sense. But still I'd keep info on her to myself.

"Oh, I just talk with her some. She's just a kid."

"OK, let it go. How about Mai. You been down to the East Hotel lately?" It was Santimaw this time.

"I stopped in some morning last week but just to play cards. There were a bunch of girls around, but none were much interested in working, even the infamous Miss Mai. We played blackjack instead." I figured I'd not tell them of my earlier visit, not now.

"You don't want your little hooch girl finding out that you hang down there, or your ass is grass with her."

"I bet she's never heard of it." Man, I want to get off this topic with these guys.

"There ain't nothing that goes on in this country that they all don't know about." It's Banks again. "They got spies everywhere for everything, not just the military. The brass in this Army doesn't know shit. These gooks work everywhere and know all the Army's business. I read somewhere once, I can read you know, that the 'Vietnamese grapevine' is the fastest form of communication known to mankind. So, that girl knows everything that's going on too."

"OK," I answered as we entered the mess hall. "Let's drop it."

It smelled great this morning. Coffee, bacon, eggs, even the fried dehydrated, re-watered potatoes looked appetizing. You can't smell 'em. They cooked eggs to order in our mess. Omelets, scrambled, anyway fried, it was great. We ate out fill.

"OK, boys, what's up today? No Ammo Dump last night so we're going to be sent out on some sort of detail. There must be some escape."

"You ever been to the Train Compound?" asked Banks. "No," I said.

"Why don't we each skip out of whatever job we're given and meet up at the main gate in an hour. If all goes well, we'll be at the pool by eleven."

"They got a pool there?" said Santimaw.

Banks replied in the affirmative, and that wasn't all by a long short, tennis courts, great bar, #1 mess, a regular officer's joint. Any luck we'd meet at the gate a little after eight and take it from there. Luckily for me, I ducked out of the radio shop after ten minutes and stopped by the hooch where Kim worked.

"Hey, Kim, how are you?"

"I am fine," she answered. I edged closer since she appeared to be alone just inside the folds of the tent. She seemed receptive so I hugged her quickly, brushing against her breasts with nipples nearly pushing through her thin silk like top.

"No, not here, Collin, I tell you come and see me after my work maybe two or three nights. Then we talk and maybe have some soda."

Leaving it at that, I said my good byes and walked along down to the front gate. As luck would have it, Easly was on. Didn't really matter during the day, but I could leave a message with him for Santimaw and Banks.

"Hey, Joseph, how's it going?"

"Great day so far," he answered. "Where the fuck you going so early?" he asked.

"Oh, I slipped out and am heading off to Bien Hoa. I'm supposed to meet up with Banks and Santimaw here but maybe you could tell them to meet me at the stand in Tam Hiep. We'll walk through the village on to the Bien Hoa Highway."

He agreed so I left and hoofed across the road, which was already crowded with every vehicle known to man. The frog pond along the village path was occupied with a couple of young boys trying to catch a few. Looked like kids anywhere that had skipped school on a bright spring day. As I walked into the square in Tam Hiep and approached the stand, I noticed someone that looked familiar.

"Aren't you Omar?" I asked. "Remember meeting on the road between Saigon and Thu Duc?"

"For sure," he answered. "Your name Collins, right?" "I told you I have girlfriend in Tam Hiep and today no work. I not busy so I come looking for her. You know Hiep? Very beautiful. For now, she my best girlfriend. She my only girlfriend. I am in the field too much with this unit, the 199th Light Infantry Brigade. Not enough time for looking for girlfriends."

"Omar, tell me about yourself. How'd you get where you are with the American Army? What part of Vietnam are you from?"

"This be long story or short story. You take pick."

"Maybe somewhere in the middle," I answered.

We grabbed a stool at the village stand and ordered an early morning beer. After all, it appeared that this was a day off and the heat was building up.

"My family came to this part of Vietnam in 1954 when the people from the North came south before the permanent division. You know what the word was, 'the blessed virgin has gone south' so my family go south. We never very good Catholic, but it looked like a good move my father say. They all go Ho Nai up road here by 199th base camp. Pretty funny I end up there. Maybe half mile from old house."

"Omar, is that why all the Catholic churches in Ho Nai? I never could figure that out."

"Hey man, we not all Buddhist and we need churches. But I like to sin, like girls."

"Yea, I get the drift, Omar. Me too."

"Do you know Kim Lon who lives down the path there in that little house? Maybe soon she will be my girlfriend."

"I know her. She friend Hiep. Very pretty girl. Very sexy. Cambodia girl have more body."

Omar went on about the qualities of different girls in Tam Hiep that he had been with over time. I was thinking that he must know more about this place than anyone that I'd talked much with so I asked him.

"What really goes on here, Omar? I never see any men other than a few old and crippled characters. No young men. Where are they all?"

He began again with another monologue. "Some go with ARVN. They drafted. Most are with other side. Everybody quiet about that because Americans have all the guns and the bombs and the money. I think we like our own people better. Same like you. The girls here like American money. Have families to feed. They like GI too, I think. Some GI. But they like Uncle Ho best."

"Come on, Omar, they can't all be VC." I wasn't sure of that but thought I'd put it forward.

"No?" said Omar smiling, "They all be VC. But no matter. We all friends in Tam Hiep."

Well, maybe the Army was right with the Off Limits ruling. However, the only trouble I ever saw in Tam Hiep was caused by the American MPs. That said something.

"Hey, Collins. Hang on." It was Santimaw. He and Banks were walking toward the stand.

I introduced them to Omar. We shot the shit for a while and then left Omar at the stand waiting for Hiep as we walked toward the Bien Hoa Highway and the way into town. We jumped the first Lambretta that came along, stopped at the laundry in Tan Mai where some enticing girls were occasionally available, thought better of staying and continued on to the Hope Bar. It was nearly empty, pretty early in the morning too, but the 173rd must have been out of town or they'd have been represented. Khan was on the job.

"What you want, GI, more money? Why you no come and see Kanh for long time?"

"We very busy my friend Kanh." I answered. "And we want to spend money, not like before. You know Bob and this other guy be Santimaw."

"How you say, Santimaw?" she asked. This took some doing but was worked out. Banks started in once again with his pickup methods, which had absolutely no effect on this girl. She was all business and that business was running this bar. "If you want that you go somewhere, not here, OK. What you drink?"

We ordered another round of 33s, the standard fix for thirst anytime of day or night just about anywhere in Vietnam. "Where Tam" I asked, thinking that Santimaw might like come company. "She no work this early in the day," said Kanh. "You can all talk with me and you can all buy me a tea."

"One tea for Kanh." I said , "these guys are Cheap Charlies Kanh, and won't come up with much. I'll pay for the beer and the tea. Let's talk. What's up with the 173rd?" I asked.

"They tell me that major parachute jump over near the Cambodia border, but I already know that before. My sister work at Brigade Headquarters and she tell me."

"How much before the GIs tell you?" I asked, curious about the current speed of the "Vietnamese Grapevine." Before she could answer, Banks joined in with "These fuckers know everything before we do."

Kanh chimed in viciously "If you talk # ten about people of Vietnam you go, di di mau right now."

I offered a quick apology and told Banks to shut the fuck up. He genuinely likes the people here but can't get a grip on his quick lip. Santimaw was smiling.

"I've had the same problem with the Mexican farm workers when we're baling hay west of Sacramento. You gotta try and be smooth, Banks, even if it goes down hard. It's easier that way."

They went back to talking about doings in the Company while I small talked with Kanh. One beer appeared to be enough, so we left and started walking.

"I've got an idea," said Santimaw, "Let's go look up Mai Ly. I could use a good workout."

I chimed in with I don't know about that. I'm trying to get something going with the hooch girl Kim Lon.

"Big fucking deal," said Banks, "what's that got to do with fucking around down here. Shouldn't be any different than back home. And who the hell do you think you are anyway, getting fixed up with a gook girl. Shit man, what the fuck."

"You don't need to make fun of me. I need a girlfriend. I'm getting tired of all this short time girl bull shit. I'd like a girl to talk to maybe, not just screw. What the fuck man."

"I'll tell you what," said Santimaw, "You guys are both full of shit. Let's stop in and see what goes down. Who knows, she might not even be there."

We left it at that, but I was thinking about Kim Lon as we walked along. I liked just talking with her. She had more English than most girls here. Quite frankly, I never was able to get much of a conversation going with any of the "round-eyed" girls I knew back home either. You gotta start somewhere and I wanted to start with her. I'd heard about Mai Ly and was a little skeptical. Her methods as predicted by these fuck heads were beyond any sexual experience known to me.

"Let's look her up then. Anything new, sex wise, has to be an improvement."

It turned out to be a bit of a walk. Almost as far as the MP lockup off the main square downtown Bien Hoa.

"I think it's down this alley here," said Banks. "I was here for the works a few weeks ago."

"How come you didn't ask me along then," I asked.

"Well, shit man, I thought it might be a little too much for you to handle. You remember those girls on Christmas?"

Yes, I remembered "those girls." They were deaf mutes. I wasn't too proud of that, but they did need the money I figured, so it must have been OK. Mai Ly was a grown up, almost an old woman it was reported. She was at least thirty.

As luck would have it, Mai Ly was in house. An ordinary-looking middle-aged Vietnamese woman at first glance, so I was wondering what the attraction was as she washed what appeared to be a long, narrow rag with knots on it. Santimaw said he'd take a break. He said he'd worn himself out late last night with a hooch girl who stayed behind. Banks was in tight conversation with another girl who worked in this joint, so I was elected to undergo the Mai Ly experience.

We retired to the usual, a bed with old sheets on wires surrounding it.

"I am Mai Ly. What your name?" she asked. "My name Collins, Bill Collins." I answered.

It was last names over here with everyone, GI or short time girl. After all that's what was printed on most fatigues.

"Ok, Collins, you take off clothes." I did as directed and asked her why she did not do it as well. She indicated that it would not be necessary.

So I laid back ready to partake in the pleasures of Mai Ly as she grabbed me by the pecker. Then she started licking it and sucking a little bit and then she moved down to my balls and resumed the same. And then she moved down to my bung hole and started in on that.

"Hey, what you do?" I asked, as she inserted her tongue a bit inside and then worked around at the circumference with her finger. Then came out the knotted rag.

"Hey, what that?" I asked once again as she started stuffing it up my ass, one knot at a time as she sucked away. I didn't know what the hell this was all about, but it felt damn good as she again began licking and sucking away. It was beginning to feel better and better. She kept stuffing and licking, stopping once or twice to see how I was doing, and I was able to reply that all was right with the world. Gradually, a faint memory of something like this brought me back to the Kama Sutra and the Golden Balls, which I didn't think much about at the time of its reading. This was beginning to be the real thing, and let's face it, a Vietnamese short time house couldn't afford any golden balls.

"How you go?" she asked.

"I almost go," I answered.

Very shortly, the spasms began. Each squirt was worth one knot until the squirts weakened, and suddenly, Mai Ly yanked the whole damn rag out in one quick shot, knots and all. I almost passed out and wasn't able to speak for a time. She asked if she was number one.

"Yes, for sure." I answered as I caught my breath. "You are number one girl even if the boys say you are an old girl."

"No, I not old." she said. "I very young. You come back to see Mai Ly again, OK."

I was thinking that this one time might be enough. I did tell her however that sometime I would be back for a visit, knowing that it was time for that girlfriend, for Kim Lon, for sure. Maybe enough of this.

As I pulled on my fatigues, the image of Linh reading her *Paris Match* at the Gala Bar in Saigon entered my brain. I had to look her up soon, and there was a chance I could get the evac run to Cholon tomorrow. Maybe I could have two girlfriends and skip Mai Ly in the future. Not that she wasn't a good girl.

"Collins, let's go get some food. I'm getting hungry." It was Santimaw who had awakened from his nap in one of the back stalls. Banks too was ready to get moving. It looked as if his short time had morphed into a long time, so they were trying to adjust the price. He might have coughed up another two bits.

"Let's hit the Bien Hoa Club." I said.

"Fuck me, that's for lifers," said Banks. "And I ain't no lifer yet. And I might add that one of 'em from the company might be there. What then?"

"You've got a point." I answered, "but let's check it out. If it looks clear, we'll get a steak, if not, down to the market."

A quiet morning in Bien Hoa, though it was approaching noon.

"You ever notice that the only males visible seem to be kids, teenage toughs, old men and cripples, or cops and ARVN troops. There's about none from eighteen to fifty."

Santimaw shrugged. This wasn't the kind of topic that interested him. Banks said "If you can't figure it out by now, Collins, you're as dumb as all these fucking lifers who run this man's Army. They're all VC, one way or another. Who wouldn't be? If some asshole bombed my house or my friends or my neighbors, he'd be an enemy forever. And I'll tell you another thing, which you probably won't like very much. If some gooks were over in my town fucking all the young girls, I'd kill their asses in a minute. So you figure all these gooks here are going to be patriotic Americans, you'd better figure again. We're fucked here. I hope it don't take too many years for all those brilliant, educated patriots who run our country to give the order to vacate this fucking fiasco. Though myself, I'm in no rush, I kind of like it here."

"That's quite a mouth full, Banks, more than I've heard from you before." He was right, no doubt. It's looked that way to me since pulling into Camp Alpha. I was kind of liking it here myself, if you just didn't look too far...or think too far.

The Bien Hoa Club could possibly have been a left over from the days of the French War. It was located down along the Dong Nai River, which ran along the edge of town just below the market. It was not frequented by GIs for the most part. Officers, NCOs and civilian government workers made up the clientele but very few local Vietnamese.

The route from Mai Ly's joint to the Bien Hoa Club went through half of the city. Past the square that had the best noodle stand in town and past the East Hotel and the market. As we left the market, I asked if either Banks or Santimaw had heard anything of the operation going on in the Iron Triangle, Operation Cedar Falls.

"Bertzik has already been out there picking up tanks that have been blown up," said Banks. "He said it didn't look good. Quite a few guys were killed so far. You must have read what Johnson said about it."

"No, I haven't," I said.

"According to the 'Stars and Stripes' President Johnson's statement, 'by the time we get done with it, a crow would starve to death flying over'. That's what I read," said Banks.

Santimaw pipes in "They're all full of shit. I hear they got tunnels all over the place in that area. It's not too far from Cu Chi, is it?"

"Maybe so, but if they get the Roman Plows out like they had in the Ammo Dump clearing it out after it blew the last time, they'll do some damage. They might spray the piss out of it too and that doesn't even count the B-52s. You could hear 'em the past couple of nights. At least I could." It was a faint rumble, but I was sure it was them. Some guys in the hooch who have been here most of a year let me know. They said that at times, the rumble was much closer.

We were coming up on the club. I stepped ahead to get a look inside to be sure it was safe. As luck would have it there, big as shit was SGT Judd along with SGT Barbara both wolfing down steaks it looked like.

"Not today, boys; both sergeants are here. We're going to have to go to the market, maybe to the duck place. They got good prices. Duck, noodles, and beer for a buck. You can't beat it."

"Fuck me, I wanted a steak," said Santimaw. "Fuck the Duck."

"It doesn't matter," said Banks. "This'll be cheaper. I didn't want to spend for a steak anyhow, we never do at home. Too much money."

"You rednecks down in Arkansas should be eating some beef. All them Chitlins and chicken won't keep you going."

"We don't eat Chitlins, you ass hole, that's nigger food. Ain't no White man down my way ever tasted them."

"Then how the fuck do you know they're no good?" came back Santimaw.

"Can we cut the bull shit and get on with the duck? I need a beer."

Eventually, we were able to partake of the duck and the beer. No complaints. As we were leaving, it occurred to me that we should stop in at a little stall in the corner of the town market. There was a quiet beautiful girl there who sold what she called Spanish fly. The real interest was talking with her. It wasn't just her beauty. It was the way that she promoted the "product."

"OK," said Banks, "we'll humor you. Don't you have any beautiful girls up North. It's all you talk about."

"It's not all, and we do have some lookers up North, but why pass the vision of a beautiful girl. This one's a vision, I'm telling you."

When we stopped in, there were no complaints. The boys were gawking.

"You remember me?" I asked. "My name Collins. I forget yours."

"My name Toi. Before I show you Spanish fly. You want to see now. Maybe your friends or maybe you want buy."

I said possibly but that she'd have to talk more about it. So she began.

"This Spanish fly very good for making love long time. You rub it on the end of your dick and you make any girl crazy for love. Make love all night."

"Can you rub it on the girl too?" asked Banks with a sneaky grin trying to trip her up.

"Ah, yes. Can rub between girls legs, on her nipples, everywhere."

I think Banks and Santimaw appreciated the girl's looks and her explanations of Spanish fly, but enough was enough, and we said so long and began looking for a Lambretta for the ride back to the Company. It was late enough in the day to sneak a nap in before beer time at the club if none of us had been missed.

There were no problems back at the Company. They flopped down on their cots, but Pacheco and Crow, two troops from the radio shop had just finished up work so were heading for a beer at the Company club. Both of these guys were a gas. And diametric opposites.

Pacheco hailed from New Bedford. He and his father dealt with the local mob, but one morning, he discovered his father in their car trunk with twenty bullet holes in him. Pacheco left town for the Army and hadn't been back since. Crow, an Appalachian boy from West Virginia, only nineteen but looking forty was known company wide as the Baldheaded Kid.

One side of his chest had been kicked in by a mule. He did look forty, but both of these guys were good troopers.

Pacheco asked me if I had heard about Easly. I hadn't seen him since the choppers went down a couple of weeks ago and told him so.

"Well, he bought the farm," said Pacheco.

"No…how the hell." There hadn't been much going on around here the past couple of weeks, and any ammo dump incidents spread like wildfire.

"He was up with the 11th Armoured Cav. in Xuan Loc working on an APC radio transmitter out on an operation, and they hit a mine. Bertzik just hauled the APC back here for the junk yard and spread the word. A fucking bad break, that's for sure."

Easly's death put a damper on the beer drinking for me, so I wrapped it up for the day. We never did make it to the Train Compound.

CHAPTER 6

LAST night I slept with Kim Lon. It was a very brief coupling for an unexpected reason. Kim had a child, a little girl who began fussing; I had thought this child had belonged to one of the neighbors; however, it turned out that she wasn't one of the village kids; she lived here with her mother.

"I had this long-time boyfriend," she began, "who say he will marry me. When he go home I am with baby four months. He say that when he finish in six months, he will return to Vietnam and get job with RMK BRJ. So I have baby and I wait for him. I wait and I wait, but he never return. I cry for him, and I cry and I cry, but I never hear from him again. Then I be angry. I never want to be with GI again. I never have until tonight. Maybe with you, it be OK. But I don't want husband now."

Quite frankly, I took Kim for a young village girl with little sexual experience. It turns out she's way ahead of me. I was a good four years older, and pretty "pussy green," but just like her, I wasn't looking for a mate this early in the game.

"It's OK, Kim. We can be good friends now. I need a friend like you. One as beautiful as you."

She liked that. I mean what girl doesn't. I like kids too. Kim's daughter's name is Hoa.

I asked her how she was able to raise her child and yet work all the time.

"My friend Mama San next door help me. She take care of many children. I work for GI every day and wash clothes at night, and I have to go to Cambodia every month to give money to my father. He old man and cannot do much work. So you see I very busy."

I commiserated with her and then started thinking, fantasizing really.

"Do you stay for a long time when you go to Cambodia?" I asked her.

"Just one night. Maybe you go with me some time. I show you Phnom Penh."

"Sure, maybe I can do." That was food for thought. Who knows, but I'd be sticking my neck out, that's for sure.

We were driving along to Saigon with the evac run from the radio shop. I lucked out again and had Banks with me riding shotgun. We were set for a good day. SGT Hanna who ran the shop didn't seem to be aware that if we left at seven, we could be back by one all things considered. It usually took us till at least six. Time for a tour.

"Collins, let's pull over at the car wash. We're early," said Banks.

There were half a dozen car washes along the route to Saigon, but oddly, none of them offered a wash. Just beer, cokes, dope, and girls. Maybe noodles. It was a good way to kill an hour or so, but I had been in contact with my old friend Paul at the 4th Military Intelligence Battalion, and we were to meet up at the Kangaroo Bar.

"Next time, Banks. We've got an appointment in Saigon. The Kangaroo Bar, if you know where that is."

"OK, fuck it. That sounds good."

We were slowed down along the highway where it Y-ed off to Di An, the home of the Big Red One, the army's 1st Infantry Division. Operation Cedar Falls was winding down, and Junction City was gearing up, and a large convoy was forming along the shoulder of the road near that interstation.

I'd found a new way to contact Paul besides using the mail that was too slow for the times, because I never knew when or how I would be by. We'd gotten a new company clerk, a guy named Carl Mooers who had shipped in from Germany.

He seemed like a straight guy and offered to ease things in the Orderly Room for me if I ever needed a favor. I offered to show him the works here in Vietnam, for whatever that was worth. I also asked him why he would transfer here from Germany.

"I'm sick of those old whores in the windows of Amsterdam," he answered. "Heard there was some good pussy over here in old Nam and didn't figure there was much chance of being shot as my MOS is Clerk Typist."

He figured that right, and he made the army phone system available for me to contact Paul who had a similar relationship with the 4th MI Orderly

Room. If you pay attention, there can be a good deal of freedom in this man's Army.

Traffic was picking up as we approached the Newport Bridge, the main approach to the city. The smaller vehicles were the most difficult to deal with. Of course, the carts powered by horses and the occasional oxen were also a problem. Too much so, once in the city.

"Watch it," Banks yelled. "You almost ran over the old guy on the bike."

"Where the hell is he? I still don't see him."

"He's behind us now," said Banks, "Take the next left. It's shorter and less traffic."

The evac run connected our radio shop with a higher echelon operation still run by the military in a revamped rice mill in Cholon, the Chinese part of Saigon. If they couldn't fix it, on the next pickup, we'd drop it off at a PA&E complex where civilians worked on electronics. If they couldn't fix it, the next stop was a local Vietnamese contractor who had a couple of kids working out back on the concrete who could usually take care of the problem. This is one reason I wondered why the Americans ever thought they could win the war. We were up against brains with a cause. Ultimately, bombs can't compete.

While driving along the river, I noticed the Majestic Hotel, which I knew was at the foot of Tu Do Street. It's be easy enough to stop in at the Kangaroo on the way home. Hope Paul got the message.

"Can we stop in at the Capital Hotel for some good chow?" asked Banks as we drove by. For me, this was the border of Cholon. Who knew the exact boundary, which didn't matter for a hill of shit anyhow.

"I'd really rather not, Banks. Fuck it, man, why be difficult. I told you I gotta meet up with a friend on Tu Do Street, and the sooner we get there, the better chance of that. We can always eat at that super Army chow hall some other run. It ain't gonna go anywhere."

We were able to unload our malfunctioning radios and transmitters without much fuss and had nothing to drop off elsewhere, so we headed back upcountry fairly early. There was one comment from the GI who handled our paperwork.

"Why the fuck do you guys keep dropping off those prick twenty-fives (PRC-25s) that have bullet holes in them. We can't fix the fucking things, same as you guys. Just junk 'em."

The prick twenty-fives were back pack radios. The trooper wearing it on his back was the prime target during an ambush. Without the radio, no air could be called in. There couldn't have been too many volunteers for that job.

The problem with a deuce-and-a-half in Saigon was where do you park it? It would be possible to leave it in the compound at the 4th MI if we were up in that part of town but not here on Tu Do St. We had driven past the Majestic, round the circle and up Ha Ba Trung to the Opera House, thought about leaving it in front of the Continental and then decided to leave it in front of the Air France office below the Caravelle on Tu Do, which was not far from the Kangaroo.

"I'll keep track of it," said Banks. "You go see if your friend is here. I don't mind sitting up on the hood watching the world go by."

"Don't you mean, Banks, 'watching the pussy walk by'?"

"You got it," he said. "Bring me a beer, and I'll sit here as long as you want."

I agreed to that good deal. As luck would have it, Paul was in the Kangaroo talking to Sandy. Neither of these guys was ever at a loss for words. I greeted both the boys and had Tot send out a beer for Banks. Paul was telling Sandy about a recent episode up in Cu Chi.

"Usually up there, I'm in the back of Bird Dog or sitting on the floor in the doorway of a Huey scouting out whatever they want me to identify. This time I went out with a company on patrol, which in no way is my MOS. Luckily, I wasn't in the lead. That poor guy got plugged and went down fast before we had arrived where they were going to use my expertise , which I think was bull shit all along because 'what the fuck' they all got eyes as good as mine. A truck or a spider hole looks the same to all of us. Anyhow, I didn't get hurt and beat it back to Saigon soon as I could."

"I don't think we even have people like you in the Australian Army," said Sandy. "We were mostly on foot in my unit in Vung Tau. A couple of jeeps and a couple of trucks. Otherwise, 'fuck me dead,' mates, you Yanks got so much of everything you never know what to use in a scrap. All we diggers need is a rifle and some get go."

"Come on, Sandy, we're OK too. How about Flynn, you seen him around?" I asked.

"He was home for a couple of days after we met here the last time, but since then, I haven't seen him. Those photographers can go anywhere they feel like in this whole theatre just like that. All they have to do is find an empty seat and go to it. He takes assignments from other publications besides *Paris Match*. Probably got sent out to some fire fight. He loves that shit."

We shot the breeze a bit, Paul and Sandy didn't seem to need me to keep the conversation going, so I took my leave and walked down to the Gala and look in on Linh. The bar was nearly empty it being early afternoon. She was there at the end stool, looking at the latest *Paris Match*. Man, she's beautiful. She possessed a more sophisticated beauty than Kim Lon. I mean, what the hell, she was a teacher rather than a scullery maid. I loved both, of course.

"Linh, how are you today?" The usual greeting to a girl in a bar in Vietnam. "I am fine, Collins, and how are you? You see, I remember your name."

We talked for some time. I liked to think it was somewhat above grade from the usual drivel discussed between people like me and her. I mean we were both here for one reason. To make a living, to feel you might have a friend in the world, to get drunk, and to get laid. Which was appearing to be increasingly difficult in the bar room environment. I hate to think that I'm a short time GI when I'd rather be neither. Eventually, the conversation came around to the Vietnamese political situation, believe it or not.

"Is your family from the North, Linh. I'm curious. So many people I meet in Vietnam have a story that I don't expect."

"Yes, I am born in the village of Song Tay, the same as Premier Ky. Like his family, we come to the South before 1956 when the Americans help form the Diem Government to make a country of South Vietnam. We move to Ho Nai, where I say I am from today. Only for you do I tell my true story. I go to Catholic School, learn French very well, grow up, get married, have child, husband die, get job teaching school, and I here today talking with you."

Wow, I didn't expect that kind of in-depth honest conversation.

"Linh, could you wait some, and I will bring beer to my friend in truck. Just one minute."

I grabbed a 33 and hoofed it down to the truck where Banks was still sitting on the hood watching out for girls I presumed.

"I saw a couple of foxy round eyes with big tits and great asses. Said they worked at the embassy and were heading up to the pool on top of the Caravelle. I mean, Christ Collins, I love these girls here, but a little more body ain't all bad sometimes. I ain't talking fat, I'm talking just right pussy."

"That's just great, Banks, but here's another beer. I've gotta get back to the girl in the bar before some other clown shows up."

After stopping in at the Kangaroo where Paul and Sandy were still in serious conversation, seeing that there was no need for me, I got back with Linh.

"Linh, I've often wondered if people who moved here from the North keep in touch with their relatives who stayed. Is it even possible?"

"It is, but very difficult," answered Linh. "When my husband was alive, and he was a Captain in the VNAF, we had better luck. Almost everyone in South Vietnam has someone in the NLF or the VC as you GIs call them. They are our friends and relatives. It is through them that we have the best chance of staying in touch with people in the North. You know Premier Ky from my village of Song Tay has people there, and he must keep with them. When all this war ends, we will be together again sometime."

"You sound like they will win." I said, a little shocked in a way since she spoke so matter of factly.

She smiled before asking "What you think?"

I smiled too, thinking that perhaps we'd better change the topic to love making and I tried but got nowhere, so finally bade her farewell saying that I would return soon and stopped in once again at the Kangaroo being sure that Banks was still occupied looking at pussy from the hood of the truck. Thank God for Arkansas. The boys were still talking. Paul never stops once he gets going, so I pulled a stool up beside Kanh to find out what the deal was today at the Kangaroo or if there was any news or gossip that might be interesting.

"What's up, Kanh?" I asked. She had the look in here eye of a girl who was up for anything with anyone.

"What you want?" was her reply.

"Kidding, we just talk. Business slow today."

"All GIs busy with Junction City. Ones who come here, they no fight, but they say they are still busy. I tell them about that operation before they know so they say I VC. I no VC, I smart girl…and I survive, and my child survives."

There was no doubt about that but enough for politics with bar girls. If we don't get our ass moving back to the Company, we'll lose this job. So Banks and I left Paul and Sandy for the road home to Long Binh.

"Hey, Collins," said Banks, "you think we can pull into this car wash and check out the girls."

"No chance, my boy, we're late enough as it is. Let's hook up with the boys in the club after we park this truck."

CHAPTER 7

I lay in my cot beneath the mosquito net thinking. Thinking about Kim Lon. Thinking about what I'm doing here. Thinking about going nowhere fast. Last night in the Ammo Dump, while playing it safe and lazy on the reaction team; heavy fire was heard on the eastern front. We were called to "react" and all hell broke loose. We could see the tracers as we loaded in a deuce-and-a-half to reach the perimeter on the eastern edge. As we drew closer, only US fire was apparent by tracer. The VC are normally in and out so fast that that's probably what's happening here. They don't hang around for any air or artillery to be called in.

The firing stopped; however, screaming could be heard so that wasn't good. When we drew nearer, the medic with us from the 199th jumped off and ran toward the screaming. As I closed in, I recognized Wilton from the 25th Infantry who'd been with me on patrol there weeks earlier.

"Christ, Collins," he said, "You wouldn't believe it. The bastards snuck in and turned our one claymore toward us and then popped off a couple of shots. The guys on guard upfront set off the mine, and it nailed them. They looked pretty fucked up, but this medic seems to be on top of it. I'm sick of this fucking place, man, I want to get back up to Cu Chi. As fucked up as it is there, at least I know the place."

I tried to calm him down, but there was nothing more to do. A good medic did it all. In a short time, a Dustoff dropped in and took the wounded over to the 93rd Evac. The medic was sure they'd all make it. I'm still here under the mosquito net trying to get a nap after being awakened for the reaction team all night. I'd hoped to be heading off to Bien Hoa early, but it isn't going well. Too much movement last night. I stopped in at the mess hall, which still had hot coffee and cold fried eggs that were quite tasty and made not for a bad breakfast. Kim Lon was working at her regular hooch, so I stopped in to see her on the way to the main gate.

"Hey girl, how are you?" I said after peeking in the hooch, making sure no GIs were inside.

"Hey, GI, how you do?" she answered. After a bit of joshing and flirting, we agreed to get together in Tam Hiep two nights from now.

It was a nice day. Not so hot with an almost blue sky. Peaceful. I was hoping that the guys messed up last night were doing OK at the hospital. Maybe I'd check in tonight to find out, though I didn't know them. They too were with the 25th from Cu Chi.

I walked up to the Vung Tau intersection where the highway Y-ed off to the right. There were a number of girls dressed up on the corner, some with their families, waiting for their lovers. Or so, they thought and hoped. Often times, it turned out like Kim Lon, they didn't show or worse yet they showed but never returned. A couple of GIs were there though with their duffle bags. This was the corner near the turn off to the 90th Replacement Company where most GIs shipped in to and out of Vietnam. You'd see the girls crying at times. Maybe as the soldier was leaving, or maybe because he didn't show up. Maybe he had left the day before. It was a dirty deal all around. You lived for the day here, as did the girls; but on occasion, there was a future to be dealt with. I couldn't watch it and turned left toward Bien Hoa. It was still a nice day, and I was open for anything.

Shortly, a Lambretta slowed so I flagged him over and jumped on. No one else aboard. Some of the girls were hanging laundry as we passed through Tan Mai, so I jumped off for another cup of coffee and to jabber a bit with them. They were all hard workers but loved talking and flirting as they worked. The ironing was done with the old cast iron types that were heated up on charcoal stoves, and during this season were hung out on dozens of lines to dry. During the wet season, it must have been a trip to dry everything, mostly fatigues.

I wasn't awarded much of a reception. They were busy after all so I said the hell with it and started walking. It was either Miss Mai at the East Hotel, Mr. Vann at the USAID office or the swimming pool at the Train Compound. All were great possibilities. I'd been with Miss Mai once and she had more than lived up to her reputation as the hottest short time girl in this area. Maybe in all of Vietnam. Who knew? I'd met her first playing black jack up in the hotel with the girls. Banks was with me and swore she lived up to her reputation but wouldn't fill me in on the details. I found out the details all by myself.

I hadn't met Mr. Vann yet at the USAID office down near the river. A couple of times I checked in to see if there was any volunteer farm type advisory work available for GIs. I'd heard of that being possible from some source earlier. The girl working there was of the opinion there might be, but that Mr. Vann was handling it. He was the director of USAID for Bien Hoa Province.

In many respects, the Train Compound was heaven. It had been built during the French days and was mostly intact from that time. Tennis courts, a large swimming pool that often times had white girls in bikinis lounging on the decks. Drinks were available nearby, and if lunch or dinner was ever desired, that too was available…for a price. That's how it worked here. There weren't many lowly enlisted types around. But man, they had steaks to order and a salad bar, which I'd never seen before, hick that I was. The bar upstairs served great mixed drinks for a quarter. The beer still a dime. You couldn't beat those prices.

I'd been told that the Train Compound was headquarters for the Phoenix Program in this area but wasn't able to confirm that. It's supposed to be a secret operation.

However, as it wasn't yet ten o'clock, I figured I might be able to catch Mr. Vann before he took off for the day as was usually the case. It took me awhile to find the place, it being located just a bit off the curb along the river street. A friendly looking woman was standing outside smoking a cigarette.

"How's it going?" I asked, "Does Mr. Vann happen to be in?"

"You lucked out today," she answered, "he's in the back somewhere."

I looked around inside and found him looking through a file cabinet. He looked up as I approached.

"Who are you looking for?" he asked. "I mean what can I do for you. I'm busy as hell at the moment."

"I'm looking for you, I think, if you're Mr. Vann." "OK shoot," he said.

"My name's Bill Collins. As you can see, I'm with the Army, over in Long Binh. Someone in the company told me that a couple of months ago, there was a notice out from USAID that they were looking for persons with a farm background to help with the Vietnamese in the countryside. I was hoping that something was still going on in that regard and that maybe they'd want me. I heard you run USAID in Bien Hoa."

"Yes, I do. I'm in charge of all military and civilian advisors in III Corps. You off the farm?" he asked.

"Yup, right off the farm. Been milking cows and all that goes with it since I was ten years old. Up in NY State, just north of the Adirondacks."

"That's somewhere between Saratoga and Montreal, isn't it?" he asked.

"That's right, mister, but closer to Montreal. We're an hour south."

"Why the hell were you milking cows when you aren't that far from the best racetrack in the States? That ain't too bright."

Now I don't know if this guy is kidding me or making fun of me or what the hell, but I tell him we had horses but not for the track. "Just milking cows, putting up hay and grain and whatever else goes with it."

"I know the score," he said smiling. "Just checking you out. I grew up in Virginia. How do you like Vietnam? How about the people? I've had soldiers in the past, but they seemed to just want to get out of getting shot. Nobody would stay in the countryside overnight. Pretty hard to get them trusting you when you don't dare to stay with them overnight. And by the way, it's easier to get shot out in my territory than in Long Binh, I can vouch for that. My car has more than a few bullet holes in it."

"I like everything about Vietnam, the country and the people; but the Army is getting boring. I'm just looking for a change. Looking for something to be useful at. I know farming so I figured I could be of some use. That's about it."

"Well, I've got bad news for you. Until a couple of days ago, it could have been arranged, but the word down from Westmoreland is that he can't spare any men. I'd call that bull shit of the first order, but he's the boss. Sorry, can't do anything about it."

"Tell you what, Collins, how about I take you for lunch? We'll go to the Train Compound and get a T bone. You ever eaten there?"

I told him that I'd just walked through it before, but that I'd sure like to try one of those T Bone steaks. Hell, this was working out well. We decided to walk as it wasn't a great distance. On the way, he was telling me that while he was in charge of all the civilian and military volunteers, he was also deputy commander of CORDS as well as the Phoenix Program. I wasn't that aware of exactly what those programs were but realized that Mr. Van was some kind of big shot.

When we finally were sitting in the mess hall, which actually resembled a restaurant, and digging into those T bones, he began talking of his wife and kids back in the States. Then it came down to the local girls. Turned out, this guy was a horn dog.

"Tell me, Collins, you got any hot girl friends here in Bien Hoa? You ought to, because there sure as hell are some."

I exaggerated about some of the short time girls I'd run into but said nothing of Kim Lon. That was my business, and I wasn't inclined to hear some cheap talk about her. Actually, he wasn't negative about the local girls; it was just that he had a lot of them, or so he claimed.

All in all, he was a good guy, and it's too bad it wouldn't be possible to work with him. After he left, I hung out for a while around the pool. As luck would have it, a couple of White girls showed up in bikinis. Both of 'em were knockouts. After a few beers, I finally got up enough nerve to introduce myself. The redhead worked at the Australian Embassy and was up here visiting her American friend who worked for CORDS. From my experience thus far in Vietnam, most White girls didn't make much effort talking to enlisted men. They preferred officers or civilians.

"How are you girls?" I asked. "My name is Bill, Bill Collins. As you can see, I'm in the Army here."

"No kidding," said the pretty one. "Just kidding," she then said laughing. "My name is Holly. My friend here is Leeza."

Leeza looked my way and smiled, keeping quiet. Holly being quite talkative began telling me all the details of working in the Australian Embassy located in the Caravelle Hotel in Saigon, which mostly entailed the various parties she'd attended and all the big shots she'd met. I didn't mind. It sounded interesting, and it was great just looking at her.

"Where do you live in Saigon, Holly?" I asked looking for more conversation.

"Now I'm living in the Caravelle Hotel, but we might be getting a villa soon."

"You ever met Flynn, the photographer? He lives just around the corner from you." I asked.

"Oh yes, he comes to the embassy parties sometimes. One time I went to the Kangaroo bar when he was there, but we girls aren't encouraged to make the Saigon bar scene. He is beautiful but has a Chinese girlfriend from San Francisco I'm told. Can you believe that, with all the Vietnamese beauties around this town? I don't know him very well, just to say hello so far, but who knows?"

I'm thinking I'd better just keep talking small time with such heavy competition. This Holly girl could be fun. Leeza didn't have much to say, but she did smile at me. They had to leave after checking the time, Leeza back to work and Holly had to catch her ride back to Saigon. I was hoping I'd run into them again. I'm supposed to hook up with Paul at 4th MI soon, and we were thinking of dropping in at the old Olympic Pool a short way from Tan Son Nhut. So who knows? I figured I'd go back and look into the guys who had been wounded last night in the Ammo Dump.

The 93rd Evacuation Hospital was crowded with casualties from the various units involved in Operation Junction City, which I'd heard had pretty much decimated War Zone C where the action was taking place. War Zone C was north and north-west of the Iron Triangle, which had just previously been decimated by Operation Cedar Falls. Johnson famously stated "that when he was through, a crow would starve to death flying over it," and by the time the troops, the Rome plows, the sprays, the B-52s, and other assorted aircraft were finished, I'm sure he was right. Bertzik had been up there a couple of days ago with his ten-ton picking-up burned-out tanks and that's how it looked to him.

At any rate, I eventually located the two guys from the 25th who had been wounded by the claymore last night, and luckily, both were alive and in one piece. Walking through the ward, I couldn't say the same for the other patients. Junction City was the largest operation of the war thus far with units from the Big Red One, the 11th Armored Cav, The 173rd Airborne, The 199th Light Infantry Brigade, etc. There was no end to it. By the time I left that ward, it was apparent that many limbs and faces had been lost and who knew the number of KIAs (Killed in Action).

After that scene, I immediately departed for the club and downed a few beers. All the boys were there.

"Where the hell you been?" asked Pacheco. "I know you fucked off 'cause I've seen nothing of you all day."

"I had some things to do in town that wouldn't interest you but did meet a couple of hot numbers at the Train Compound pool. White girls." I said.

Pacheco was the first to say that he had no preference. "Pussy is Pussy and that's about all I care about living here in this man's army."

I must admit it's difficult to find any other topic of conversation, but we must try. "What about food, Pacheco, I know you love food."

"I just told you, pussy, eat pussy. That my food man," he said laughing, knowing himself that he'd never turn down a morsel of food, and certainly no girl.

And then Crow, the bald-headed kid, piped in, "I don't eat no pussy. I just breed 'em."

"When I get a Mexican girl up on top of a load of hay, I do anything with her she'll let me," said Santimaw. "Anything."

Washington, like many of the Blacks, didn't approve of cunnilingas, not needing it according to him. "With a dick like mine, the girl don't want nothing when I wrap up a session with her."

Carl, the clerk from Germany, piped in, "I'm into it I'll tell you, but some of those old girls in the windows in Amsterdam been working at it twenty or thirty years, and I lost my appetite. Now, a young hooch girl, that's something else."

I left, not waiting for a reply from Banks who would more than likely have topped them all, perhaps with his favorite joke.

"I'd like to break her down like a shot gun and horse fuck her." A real classy line.

Or possibly, "I'd like to get that little man in the canoe and beat him severely around the head and shoulders with my tongue."

I never mention Kim Lon to these guys now, not wanting to hear them downgrade my budding relationship to the run of the mill "short time." Not that I've got anything against those girls either.

Back in the tent, I was lying under the mosquito net thinking. Once looking out over Dang Da St. with Paul from the roof of his barracks in Saigon, I noticed a number of small horses being led down the street. They were sleek and fine boned. Paul then mentioned that we weren't so far from Phu Tho Racetrack. Someday I'd like to stop in there and see how they race in the East. I lived close enough to the track in Saratoga Springs to make the races once in a while and of course we raised horses on the farm. Just hadn't made it to that level yet.

CHAPTER 8

THIS ammo dump detail is getting old. Tonight, of all things, I was stuck on the entrance where the ordinance was trucked in from the docks in Cogido. There must have been a shortage of army trucks because local Vietnamese truckers were handling it. Nothing wrong with that, but the problem was these trucks were of every make and type known to man. Most could carry but one pallet of ammo; consequently, there were a huge number of trucks on the job. The guards were supposed to guarantee that nothing was brought in that could cause an explosion. This isn't a joke. The powers that be didn't trust the truck drivers. They considered the fact that more than a few might be VC or at least sympathizers and might possibly place a homemade explosive device under one of the large pads of ammunition, certainly a distinct possibility.

More than once, inoperative charges attached to watches had been discovered on some pads. There was the possibility that sappers had crawled in at night, or the easier option was having a truck driver place one where it could ignite a pad. The problem was the trucks; all being nonstandard, each had innumerable hiding places for secretive charges. It was virtually impossible to search all of these vehicles that thoroughly. Consequently, they were hardly searched at all. Why waste your time? And quite frankly, most of the drivers were friendly and seemed innocuous enough. The biggest problem was it took all night. I was on with Santimaw who never could stay awake so wasn't able to catch much in the way of naps.

"Come on, Larry, get your ass awake. I need just a little shut eye. I'm hoping to get to Saigon to see my friend later in the morning."

"I need just a little more," he said. "Just a little more."

By the time dawn was breaking, the last truck had been passed through, and I was able to nod off for half an hour or so. No charges had been found and nothing had blown, so the night detail must have been a success.

Larry and I hoofed it over to the mess hall after returning to the company area. Plenty of bacon and scrambled eggs were left in the warmers, so the food woke me up along with many cups of coffee. Santimaw was going to bed for a few hours, he said. I still had in mind making a run to Saigon. After stopping in for a word with Kim Lon who claimed to be too busy for much conversation, I trucked along the main highway north to the 11 Field Force Headquarters. Their chopper pad across the road from their headquarters building was the busiest in the area while also offering a greater variety of destinations. While I had never been authorized to fly on a chopper, I found that most of them would take me along if they had room, sometimes just for a ride across the countryside.

I was standing on the ramp and could hear a Huey coming in for a landing. After he landed, I ran over to see where he was going and if I could ride along.

"Tan Son Nhut," he said. "Jump on and we'll get going."

No one jumped on with me but what the hell. My own ship. After gaining altitude and tracking a heading for Saigon, the machine turned back, landing where they had just left. A 'Full Bird' Colonel was waiting. He lined out the crew chief for not waiting for he was the intended passenger. Certainly, it wasn't me. It was straightened out, and I was allowed to stay with the 'Bird'. We each claimed our side of the chopper and were silent for the trip. In my experience, a colonel never spoke to a private for whatever reason. Still, a quick and free ride to Saigon on a ravishingly beautiful morning flying over the greenest of green countries was a joy in itself. For some reason, there were fewer bomb craters between Bien Hoa and Saigon than in the West or the Northeast.

As we flew closer to town, the chopper flew directly over what looked like the water ski site that Paul had spoken of. It appeared to be a worn down French compound along the Saigon river that had seen better days, but had a couple of outboard ski boats tied up on the shore. We intend to make it up there soon and do some skiing.

The Colonel and I parted ways upon landing at the helipad at Ton Son Nhut, and I hitched a ride to 69 Dang Da St. Paul was lying in his bunk half asleep. This was mid-morning.

"Don't worry," he said. "I've got the day to myself. Have a new job lately sleeping up at the shop. I'm on duty if any image interpreting is needed by pilots coming in after normal hours. On occasion, they've been upcountry or held up somewhere. Sometimes, infrared is used along the trail, and they're looking to pinpoint bombing in the middle of the night. Who knows why?"

"Well, I'm good for the day, so take your time. Any interesting news from home?"

"That girl I was telling you about down in the City dropped me for a new man. Probably, a fucking draft dodger, the cocksucker."

He'd told me previously that he was involved with the Vietnamese girl who worked up in his club. In fact, he bragged about nailing her on a regular basis. No charge.

"That ain't the same thing," he answered, "She's a nice girl but just for screwing."

"Hey, Paul, don't get like these other assholes. These girls are with it, and you ought to take them more seriously."

"OK, OK, let's head to the Olympic pool I was telling you about for a morning swim. They've got great diving boards. The French must have built the place."

I told him about flying over the water ski joint, and we figured we'd make it up there the next time I made it down. Ten minutes on a motor cyclo, and we were at the pool. It was all that Paul claimed including being surrounded by a twenty-feet wall, very private with a small bar and restaurant inside. There were no local Vietnamese in attendance, as per the course.

On the ride in, Paul was telling me about the previous week that he spent in Cu Chi. Apparently, the 25th Infantry used photo interpreters for their cameras, so to speak. He flew around in the rear seat of a Birddog making notes of anything visible down below that looked possibly VC or in the slightest suspicious. They took groundfire a couple of times with bullet holes in the wings, but nothing more serious. He said it beat going in the field with them on operations, which happened occasionally.

"I'm hoping I'll be able to stay with the detail I'm on," he said. "It's a match for your spot on the 'reaction team' with long days ahead. Or should I say free days."

"Both'll fit." I answered, "What the hell, we're getting close to half way through."

As luck happens on occasion, there were several White girls, round eyes in GI terminology, sunning themselves on the pool side. One of them was Holly from the Australian Embassy. We both dove in and swam to the other side where they were laid out on towels.

"She's got a great build on her, Paul, you'll see. You'll be thanking me."

"I gotta tell you though," said Paul, "I've seen quite a few of these girls around town, and they all go with Officers or civilians. Never with draftees like us."

"Hey, we're just talking. Who cares?"

Hollys spotted us and spoke to me. "Aren't you the soldier from Bien Hoa, at the pool when I was there with my friend Leeza."

"You're right, Holly. Bill Collins. This guy here is Paul; he lives down here too. This time it's me who's visiting."

"How are you girls doing?" asked Paul licking his lips. Holly's friends hardly looked at us. She's friendly enough and mentioned that she had run into the photographer Sean Flynn at the Kangaroo, her first stop there.

"It was fun. I had a great time. A number of Aussie troops from Ba Ria were drinking with him, but we had a good little visit. He's so polite. Different than our boys. I couldn't stay and hang around. Had a date with one of your compatriots from the US Embassy. We're a tight group."

I bet they are. Paul and I dove back in and swam down to the diving boards. They were five high, the top one having been blocked off because as the story went, it rose above the wall, and a GI had been shot before he could make the high dive.

We made a few shallow ones from the pool side, and I thought I'd go to the highest one and perhaps show off a little to the girls. A high-diving farmer. What did they know?

I jumped up and down on the board a couple of times and then pushed off. I pushed a little too hard but not hard enough and landed square on my back with a loud whack. I damn near passed out; it hurt so much. As I surfaced, the sound of laughter filled my ears. Still hurting, it didn't immediately register. But then I became aware the whole pool was laughing at me; even Holly. Christ, that was demoralizing. I managed to crawl out and lay alongside the pool till the pain subsided. Fuck 'em. They can keep the officers and the hot shot civilians. I'm going to stick with Kim Lon, if I can pull it off. We packed up, bought a hamburger for the road, and split. We were thinking of heading for the water ski joint, but it hurt too much, so a cyclo downtown was the obvious solution.

Paul lit up a joint as we were riding along and began talking about where he might go for R&R.

"I've heard that Australia is opening up. Some of the guys in the company are saying they've gotta go there where there's round-eyed pussy."

"Good for them," I said thinking that I'd not be sure of how to relate to a White girl who spoke 100 percent English. Quite frankly getting along, or rather more pointedly getting in bed, with girls here was a lot easier and more comfortable than my previous experience in the States.

"I don't even care if I go" I told him. "I'm getting to like it here OK. It's exciting at times, dangerous enough to make the hair stand up on the back of your neck occasionally, not that boring considering how time in the army is usually classified; not mentioning the great availability of girls, drink, and dope if you're looking for it. Not as classy perhaps as the three Bs of French Colonialism but pretty damn close. Close enough for this farm boy."

"Now, Bill, I've lived in the city. The big cheese, NY, NY. I know a lot more about women than you do. They say those Aussie girls are as hot as they come. And they are good drinkers. I hear everyone in that country is a good drinker. Also, I can talk. You're too quiet. You gotta keep the conversation going with girls. You gotta be quick and funny and get right to the bone. They know. I don't get them on my looks. It's my talking."

Now I'm thinking, it could be his talking, but I doubt it. I bet he's talked himself out of more pussy than into, and that's a sure bet.

"Ok, Paul, you take Australia, and if I go anywhere, I'll try Bangkok. It can't be much different than here."

"Forget about that for now, Bill. Where the hell are we going? We can always hit the Gala and the Kangaroo, but let's try something new. Maybe the bar on the roof of the Caravelle where all the news men go."

"Man, I'm still sore from that dive."

"You made an ass of yourself," said Paul. "Those girls are probably still laughing at us. A couple of punk GIs trying to impress sophisticated women like them, they're thinking. Hell, they can have their officers and all the rest of them. We aren't likely to be in invited to any embassy parties right off, right Bill?"

"You got that right. I'm sticking with the girl from Tam Hiep."

There was a ruckus of some sort going on as we cruised by the South Vietnamese Capital building. A few shots were fired, so we didn't slow down to check it out. The park was crowded with people down past the Notre Dame cathedral. It wasn't apparent from the appearance of the crowd what the issues were, but by and large, you didn't hear kind words for the government from any of the locals I was in touch with. Ky was running the show at the time. He picked up the job through a military takeover of the government.

"Hey, Paul, let's hit all the big shot spots, first The Continental, then the Rex, and then the Caravelle. Then we'll head down Tu Do Street."

"The beer's more expensive if you drink with the big shots," said Paul.

"It's probably 20p more, Paul, who cares!"

In a way, Paul was correct. The Continental was full of big White men or big shot White men like known journalists. The girls certainly weren't aiming for us. The best thing about the Rex was the hamburgers in the ground floor USO, though the view from the rooftop bar was good, if you were into views. We were too early for the five o'clock follies' and more than likely wouldn't have been admitted being soldiers; only accredited journalists were allowed.

If you were into views, you'd obviously stick with the Caravelle, it being the tallest building in Saigon. It's Jeanne and Juliette rooftop bar and restaurant had it all. The prices were a little more than that 20p I had mentioned, but what the hell. You only live once, even in Vietnam. I hadn't been up there in the evening when reportedly most of the photographers and journalists in Saigon were in attendance. You could see Tan Son Nhut as well as halfway to Bien Hoa or Mỹ Tho and cover the war from there. Bar room gossip filled in the rest. We decided the Kangaroo was more to out liking and that's where we ended up.

"Tot, two beers for us, please." I said to Tot. Where's Kanh? We need to talk with the girl. It be long time."

"Don't bull shit me, you GI. I know you. You see girl in Bien Hoa or Tam Hiep all the time," she replied.

I answered, "Yes, Tot, but you have such friendly girls who work here. We just want to talk. They have such good English."

Tot yelled up the stairway behind the bar "Kanh, Phuong, come here. Rich man want to see you. You come quick."

They did and Phong was quite attractive to say the least. "I want her," said Paul. "I love the pretty girl."

You had to watch the language here. Falling into what passed for the vernacular was too easy. I talked for a while with Kanh about nothing really and ordered another beer.

"How about Sandy, where's he?" I asked her. She hadn't seen him for a few days so figured he must have gone out on some sort of operation. He was involved with some type of security for the Aussi Embassy in the Caravelle so was in and out quite frequently.

"Hey, Paul, I'm stopping over at the Gala. Be back soon." Perhaps Lien was in and I'd have a drink with her.

"I'll be here. This Phuong is a really nice girl. And I don't live up in Bien Hoa."

Good luck I'm thinking, but I'm going over to see Lien. She was there but was occupied with the photographer Sean Flynn. As I edged over, it was apparent that they were speaking French. That was going to leave me out. No end to the sophistication here.

"Lien, how are you? You too, Flynn? Just stopping in to say hello."

Flynn, always the polite one said he had to leave at any rate, but not before filling me in on episode he'd had with the 25th Infantry still in Cu Chi near the end of Operation Junction City. I think he viewed himself more of a citizen of the world rather than the United States. His mother was French, and his father was from Tasmania. Perhaps that was his attachment to the Australian Army in Vietnam.

"They flattened one village between their base and the Cambodian border. Actually flattened it, mate. Drove all the people out first, though a number were killed, kids too. A bloody bad scene. They'll never win it that way. I've got to get going. See you around, mate."

Lien smiled but said nothing. "How's it going with you?" I asked. "I didn't mean to disturb you."

"It's OK, Collins. We're good friends and talk a lot. Great for my French. It's not the same as in school with the children."

While she was talking, I was looking at her. Man, this girl is beautiful. She told me how her young son was doing and how school was coming along, but I couldn't engage her in any of this bar room romantic talk. She seemed above it somehow. So, I was stumped. Back to Tam Hiep where I belonged. I stopped in up the street and picked up Paul. We returned to the rooftop bar in the Caravelle just to have a couple more beers and take in the view. It was too early for the evening news crowd.

I ate with Paul at his mess in the 4th MI and then struck out on foot hitch hiking back to Long Binh, which is a trip in itself. The main problem is knowing what vehicle is coming before jumping out from the shaded street shoulder to stick out your thumb. The last thing you want is a MP jeep, especially if you're half drunk and AWOL. I let one go by then flagged down a deuce-and-a-half.

"Where the fuck you going, man?" asked the driver. "It's after curfew and you're probably AWOL," he said with a smile on his face.

"Long Binh, and don't worry about the AWOL. None of us care." He laughed and drove on. The beauty of the ride out was the streak in the sky of a Puff the Magic Dragon. You had to see these to believe it. They were DC-3s with electric machine guns firing out the pilots side of the aircraft. These guns could fire up to 100 rounds per second with a tracer every fifth round.

We had crossed the Newport bridge not five minutes earlier when the rays were visible in the NE of the main highway. From that distance, it looked as if ray guns were firing from some kind of space ship. The firing was so fast that there was no let-up of the solid red line directly to the ground. It looked like there must be three guns in action.

"Those fucking VC are getting pounded over there," said the driver.

"Let's hope it's not a village," I answered. "I drive around the countryside up there occasionally, and it's all friendly."

"It doesn't matter," he answered, "they're all VC."

I let it go at that. Why bother? He was going to 11 Field Force Headquarters, so he dropped me off right at the company main gate. Great ride. I thanked him and walked over to the club for one last beer. Half the boys were there. Santimaw, Banks, Pacheco, Crow, even Carl from the Orderly Room.

"Carl, you're up late. This ain't Germany." I liked talking to Carl. He was more of a thinker than some of the boys.

"You can say that again. For one thing, it's so fucking hot here. Christ almighty. No draft beer either. You couldn't imagine what's available in Germany. You guys live on rusted cans of Black Label or Tiger piss or that OB from Korea. Bad stuff but at least it's cold."

"Come on, Carl, you can't beat this place, and you know it. You finished *Catch 22* yet?"

"Almost done. It reads like the Second World War was as fucked up as this place, but the book is a good read."

"I've read reviews around the time I got through it a couple of years ago. A number of them say it's really about this war. You know, the absurdity of war, all of 'em. It's becoming a cult classic among college kids, especially those who don't want to get drafted."

We shot the shit about that for a while, and a couple other books, including *The Carpetbaggers*, which neither of us figured to be of intellectual substance, not that either of us would know. After that I went back to my tent and fell asleep. A very long day.

CHAPTER 9

"YOU know, Kim, how come Vietnamese girls don't like to really kiss. They rub noses."

I was over at her little house in Tam Hiep, inching toward her bed. Kissing was difficult in Tam Hiep. I didn't mind rubbing noses, but what the fuck. It certainly didn't make old tool stand up.

"Same, same Cambodia," she answered, "but I learn to kiss from GI. I very fast learner, don't you think."

"You are number one kisser, for sure," I answered. Anything to get her into bed. Just brushing my hand across her skin was as good as kissing. It had a velvet feel, or silky or sensual. Her well-shaped, very firm breasts, with nipples that punched right on through the blouse that matched the black pajama slacks almost brought tears to my eyes. I could barely bend over by this time, so I pulled her close and kissed her hard, which she responded to in kind. Not with the hard on but a near clasp with her thighs. And a near breathless sign.

"Do you think, my sweet Kim, that we can lie down close together under your sheet and kiss some more and feel each other. Touch each other. Kiss each other everywhere." Her answer was to strip off her blouse and pants with a practiced ease. It didn't take me much longer to strip off my fatigues. I'd quit wearing socks and underwear months ago. Too complicated here… too hot.

My mind was drifting. I don't know why. I can't explain it to myself. Kim is waiting, lying peacefully on her side. It is too hot to crawl under the sheets. Not yet. Not till when? I don't know. I lie beside her and touch her skin all over and she responds by doing the same to me. With her skin, and her hands, and her lips. I'm almost losing it. It's not like the others. I run the tip of my tongue over her nipples and alternate with a wet fingertip. She even begins to moan. Most of the girls I've been with here are more sedate. They take it all in stride. They sometimes smoke, even passing the cigarette off to the girl

77

in the next bed, jabbering something in their tongue. Once a girl just pushed me aside to nurse a baby.

I don't care to think of them now. I only want to feel her. I tickle her between her legs. Her moan almost turns in to a giggle. But not quite. She is not a very tall girl. I can leave both hands with the finger tips on her moist nipples as I drop down slipping the tip of my tongue in her sex down there. The lips open up slightly, and I'm able to enter her a bit more deeply, much past the tongue's tip. I'm almost passing out as the pleasure is so intense. And I'm only inside of her with my tongue, but I need more and am able to pull myself up so that our faces touch. She has a smile on her face with her eyes half closed. I kiss her and she responds with force. I'm able to enter her. She's very moist. It slips in all the way, up to my stomach. I can't bear it; the pleasure is so great. I think is it all in my mind. How can this girl have this kind of effect on me?

We stroke away together for as long as we can. I'm hoping forever, but in not so long we both collapse in spasms, struggling for air. We stay glued together for what seems a long time. Neither of us say anything. We can't really or I can't, and she seems to be in the same place. We drift off in a kind of orgasmic slumber that I've never experienced. I don't know a great deal about this. It's not for me to say about any of it. When I come around and look at Kim, I see her looking at me with a smile on her face.

"I hope you come and see me, Bill, many times. Maybe I love you. I don't know. Maybe I do."

I'm not sure what to make of that. It doesn't matter. All of us here in this time and place live from day to day. We never know. Perhaps no one ever knows.

"You don't have to worry about me, Kim. You can't lose me. I will stay close for a long time." I meant it. Who would leave this? This feeling of absolute pleasure. All of it just for lying with this sweet, dark-skinned girl from Cambodia.

"Do you go now?" asked Kim. "You no get in trouble for sleeping with Kim. Sometimes, GI tell me that it's difficult to pass through the gate late at night."

I explain to her that I'm hoping a friend will be on guard at the gate. I don't want to leave yet. I want to lie with her longer. To sleep with her for a time. I don't want to break this spell of deep feeling, of deeper pleasure. We both fall into a deep sleep and when I awaken, I notice a slight light outside and jump up knowing that shortly SGT Judd will be holding morning formation. Kim gets up with me and we both relieve our bladders outside along the path to her house. Just like home, except the girls who visit the farm squat behind a bush. It seems in Vietnam, all bodily functions are normal. No need to hide. During the day, the girls can just roll up a pant leg. There are no public bathrooms. We rub noses to say good bye and smile at each other and then a deep kiss. I must keep her.

I didn't have a friend at the gate. There was a prick who wanted to see my pass. I told him to fuck off and walked a half mile or so to the RMK-BRJ entry point for their civilian workers. Oddly only one local man was on duty, and he waved me through without a word. It's so handy to be a White man.

"If you men don't start showing up for formation, there's going to be trouble," yells SGT Judd. I'm not putting up with this bull shit forever. Good thing you aren't in the Second World War, The Big One, The Good War, or I'd have your ass. No candy ass bull shit back then. It mattered, everything mattered. We had real men who paid attention to the importance of the war."

"Maybe we know that this isn't important," someone said a little too loudly. SGT Judd heard and looked up in disgust and said no more.

Gradually, enough men showed up, including myself in the back row, where he was satisfied, and we were dismissed to the mess hall. I was still in a daze and crawled back under my mosquito net where there was peace and privacy where I could drift off in memory of the girl Kim Lon. I could still smell her scent. I could still feel her against my skin.

"Collins, get the fuck up. What the hell you doing?" I came around as Banks was shaking the cot.

"Must have fallen asleep. Good dreams. What's going on?" I asked trying to shake the sleep out of my head.

"They need a driver for the evac run, and I said you're around somewhere and that I'd look you up?"

Thanks, Banks. I was hoping for a slow day and that should do the trick. You going to ride along shotgun?"

"That's what I'm hoping. Why do you think I'm here. That other ass hole driver would never have me along. He's a lifer and I ain't his type."

We got ourselves down to the radio shop, straightened things with SGT Hanna who had been on the job there for the past couple of weeks, filling in till a permanent E-6 transferred in with the right MOS. It took a while to load. There were a number of PRC-25s with bullet holes through them. More radio men with some real bad luck. Most of the ordinance went clear through the units.

It was a bright sunny morning, even a trifle cool considering where we were. The traffic was lighter than usual with none of the convoys of heavy military equipment that had been filling the lanes during Operation Junction City, which was winding down. Apparently, a crow couldn't survive flying over that countryside that we'd bombed and sprayed and plowed to such great affect, but the war hadn't slowed down in the least.

The view from here hadn't changed.

"Hey, Bill, how about stopping at the car wash just across the river. Even if we just get a coke or a coffee. I need to just look at the girls. There might be a real beauty serving those cold cokes in need a real man."

Before I could answer an F-100 screamed over not 200 feet above the highway and dropped a cannister of Napalm on one of the small houses along the fringe of the rice paddies on the west side of the road. Huge flames erupted from the site.

"I don't know, Banks, why are they bombing that house. Doesn't look like anything's going on anywhere near it." But then a couple of slicks slipped in from the west and dropped off two machines full of troops. Machine guns were blazing on the choppers as they landed.

There was nothing left there for them to shoot. Just ashes, I mean these houses aren't that substantial, slight wood frames with thatch sides and roofs. They seem to burn in a matter of minutes. We drove on. I didn't want to see any one get shot up. Maybe I hang around too much with the local girls.

"Ok, Collins, can we stop at the next car wash? I need a beer after that."

"I'm thinking we'd better make our way into the rice mill and drop off these radios before we get tied up along the road here. That always seems to happen, even if we're just talking."

Nothing else happened military wise till we reached the Newport Bridge. For some reason, there was an MP checkpoint. We pulled over and stopped. A couple of MPs walked over and one took a look in the back of the truck.

"So where you fuckheads heading," one of them asked, with a smile on his face. You never know for sure if a cop is kidding or not. These guys are cops after all. They turn into one automatically once the MP insignia is strapped around their sleeve.

"Down to the rice mill in Cholon where they fix these things. We don't know enough in Long Binh to handle the job." He thinks I'm kidding.

"Why the hell not," he asks. "We ain't hiring gooks to work on them are we?"

"If that's what it takes," I answered, and sometimes it did. I think SGT Judd had a point when he said that we didn't "understand the importance of it all, not like the Second World War guys."

We left the MPs and headed into the Saigon morning traffic, which was much heavier than what we'd had on the way down. As we drove along the river in front of the Majestic Hotel, we noticed a number of girls playing badminton and they looked pretty good.

"Let's stop the fuck here," said Banks. "That's what I'm looking for, nice young school girl pussy."

"You're a sick fuck, Banks, those girls are too young for people to be messing around with."

"All I can say is you Yanks don't know a damn thing. Jerry Lee's wife was thirteen when he married her."

"Yea, and it ruined him business wise. They cancelled his concerts for three years I heard. Can't we change the topic? Like drinking or something."

I will get to Arkansas someday if I get out of here in one piece. I've gotta see where this guy is from. We hung the next right and ended up with the Opera house on the right and the Rex hotel on the left. Turned too early but no way we can stop at the bars down here till we get our work done. That's the thing I found out about the army. If you do your job well and efficiently, you can get away with a hell of a lot. We hung a left, circled at the Market, and chugged along to Cholon.

The rice mill was located along a canal of moderate size, and it was possible to leave the truck there and take a cyclo down to the bar area near the Capital Hotel, a BOQ with a great mess hall that like the Train Compound required a buck to eat. It looked like the timing was right today to do just that.

"We can't stay too long Bob, if they return some of last week's load that wasn't able to be repaired here, we're going to have to run it over to the civilian Korean company that's the next step. A higher echelon repair shop. You know damn well that this man's army can't do everything. And we know for sure they can't win this damn war."

"Who cares" replied Banks. "The way things are going I might extend for another year. Great sign up bonus there for the taking. They had a re-up sarge talking with me yesterday."

"You're nuts, man, I wouldn't trust this outfit that far. You know they asked me to sign up for helicopter pilot training after basic, but you've gotta give 'em four more years or something like that. I'd have loved to learn to fly those Huey's, but I can't take a chance on it."

"You can't hardly drive a truck, how the hell you gonna fly a chopper?" Banks was smiling as he tossed that opinion out, so I didn't pay much attention. An ugly screech was heard as we were walking toward the gate. A group of GIs were standing in a circle laughing. Getting closer we could see that they had a rat tied to a cord. There was a bucket on the ground that was burning. They were lowering the rat into the bucket and he would stop screeching as he went under. Must have been fuel burning on top of water. When they pulled him back up, he was again ignited; then he yelled till they dropped him back under. I couldn't watch it, thinking it is a good thing that it was only a rat.

A high bridge spanned the canal alongside the rice mill and usually a Lambretta or a motorbike was waiting on the other side to pick up customers. Obviously, we weren't the only ones who took this way out.

We did catch a Lambretta to a bar a few blocks from the Capital Hotel and stopped in for a couple of beers. A cheap bar was available in the hotel but no bar girls. Much better company where we stopped.

We ordered T-bone steaks for dinner. "You can't beat this place," Banks said. I asked him if it was better than back home. He fessed up that he'd hardly ever been to a real restaurant in his life, just diners. I was pretty much the same. The meat was good but no better than farm beef, but I think the change of pace is what made it appealing. Fancy living for GIs.

There was an apartment that always intrigued me located across the street from the Capital. It was a second story place, painted a bright blue which was unusual for a building in Saigon. Wrought iron railings surrounded the balcony which overhung the sidewalk, which was nearly covered with an abundance of flowering vines A really pretty picture.

But that's not what filled my head. I was thinking that this must be a love apartment where someone, possibly an American officer, kept a mistress. She'd be a quiet, classic beauty from Vietnam. Every time I drive by and look up at this picture, that thought passes my mind. I was telling Banks my thoughts and his opinion were that it was just another fuck house painted up pretty. To each his own.

When we arrived back at the Rice Mill to pick up our load, we were directed to the Korean joint for some units that they had sent out and were ready for pick up. So it was back on the streets, early afternoon with a nice closure for the day ahead of us. It took a while to find the Korean business, but we did and were told to stop at another business, this one Vietnamese, for one piece that they were unable to repair. As the GIs would say "the gooks done it."

As it was located on the north side of the canal, we had to drive a ways to find a bridge, then relocate our position to place this new business. It turned out to be a couple of kids almost working under a tin roof. One of them was squatting on the ground working at rewinding armatures by hand, which I had never seen done. He had a small pile finished but what amazed me was all he had to work with was a coil of copper wire, a pair of pliers and a broken hack saw. I presumed they worked.

We picked up our piece and as we were leaving, Banks looked over at the kid who was rewinding armatures and said "we ain't gonna win this war." The kid looked up as we drove by…and kept working.

"Maybe he's VC." I said to Banks jokingly.

"It ain't no joke," he replied. "The Americans hiring VC to fix their equipment is bull shit."

We pulled in at the first Car Wash north of the Newport Bridge. This one was notable for the prime selection of girls available, not necessarily for short times but just for company, which entailed "Saigon Tea" no matter what.

"You know what, Banks, they might give me the ration man job. It'd be great. No other duty." We were talking while having some beers. Once we bought teas for two of the prettiest girls they were only interested in jabbering with each other.

"I wouldn't take that," he replied, "It's seven days a week, 4:30 till 8:30. You crazy."

"I think I can make it work. No other duty. Do the work and lay low. I'll even have my own truck."

"But we'll lose all our fun trips, like this. What the fuck you wanna do that for."

I told him it was for a change. Couldn't hurt, besides I had heard a new E-6 was coming in to the radio shop who had no slot, so they were going to make him in charge of the Evac Run. That'd be the end of me on this job.

CHAPTER 10

FOR this job, I had to leave the company at 4:30 a.m. always well before dawn when only a few Lambrettas were spread out along the main road. My first stop was down a back street in Codigo, the same area where trucks were loaded with ammunition off barges then headed to the Ammo Dump.

I was thinking that the only real problem with this job was the increased difficulty in spending the night with Kim Lon. Ordinarily, I just had to make six o'clock formation. Now I had to be back at least by 4:00 a.m. A little tight but "can do" considering the prize.

The powers that be insisted on all drivers being armed when driving this time in the early morning outside the wire. I had had no problems along those lines and expected none. All the girls I picked up for work needed the money bad to keep their families going. From conversations with them, I gathered that the word had been put out. There were seventeen or so girls and young women who met my truck at various points along the route, which after Codigo, Tam Hiep, Tan Mai, and Bien Hoa, returned through old route #1 from Bien Hoa to Ho Nai where it intersected with the main road that ran all the way to the DMZ.

I was in no hurry this morning picking up the ice and the bread, the next job on this detail, so stopped in for some coffee before heading out. Mooers, the typist from Germany, our man in the Orderly Room, was stuffing his face as usual. He could find food, anywhere.

"Hey, Carl, what's up? You hungry." He always was. Said that this mess hall was nothing compared to the ones he had available in Germany. I said I loved all the food here including the great coffee. Hell, when you think of it, and considering the availability of girls and beer and smoke, who needed great food.

"What are you reading, Carl?" I asked.

"I'm ashamed to admit it," said Carl, "*The Carpetbaggers*. It's fun man. You can't be an intellectual all the time."

"You ought to try '*The Green Berets*' and stick with the program. You know the score. Anything happening up at the Orderly Room?"

"I'll tell you what's getting to be a big deal. Fragging. You know about the other night in the NCO hooch. Some fuck head threw a smoke grenade through the door, and it apparently rolled under SGT Judd's bed. Those old lifers practically ran through the walls 'di di mauing' out of there. Lucky for them it wasn't a real grenade."

"You must have heard," I said, "where the CO and the 1st Sgt over at 66th Supply was shot last weekend by a crazy, or angry GI. Nobody saw it coming from this guy they say, but anything can happen."

"Well, Capt. Dewey has his back up and is intent on finding out who the culprit is in this company."

"Can't they take a joke. Fuck it, man, it was just smoke. There's people getting killed or almost getting killed every day over here, so what the hell's smoke. It's not a close call. It's a joke. It ain't nothing."

"Good for you to say, but Capt. Dewey doesn't see it that way. He's also worried about the guns and the drunkenness. Last night in the club, one of the yahoos from the motor pool got in a fight and went back to his hooch for his M-14. He was coming through the door of the club when one of his friends jumped him and cleared the rifle. Too many close calls for the Capt. He's gotta look out for his own self too. He's a lifer and wants to make Major."

I've got to change the subject. "Carl, have you ever read Schweizer's '*A Reverence for Life*'? It should be required reading for everyone sent over here. Especially the officers."

"I read novels man. I'm done with school. That's something you read in philosophy 101 and you ain't even been to school, a real school, a college, you know what I mean."

"In a way you're right. I flunked out after the first semester. However, I've read hundreds of books. More than all you fuckheads with college degrees."

"Hey, Collins, don't get touchy. I flunked out too, but I hope to pick it up when I get back in the world."

"Who knows," I said, "maybe I will too."

Eventually, I was able work out times to be with Kim Lon. I had to pick up ice and bread from a PA&E contract bakery, wet rations every morning, dry rations every other morning and condiments one afternoon a week. Consequently, on the "off dry" days from ten thirty in the morning till seven thirty in the evening I had a truck and free time. Sometimes, I would head over to Kim Lon's mid-day. All Vietnamese take a couple hours off for siesta time, it's so hot. And it was hotter still on occasion in Tam Hiep underneath Kim's sheets. Heaven on earth. We coasted along like this for some time.

While driving out the gate a few days later, the guard spread the word that one of the KP trucks had been shot up. The driver was badly wounded and a couple of the girls had miner flesh wounds.

"Where's you rifle?" he asked, "I'm not supposed to let any unarmed vehicle out these gates. Orders, so you better go back and get it cause you ain't coming through here without being armed."

"Come on man, I don't have time. I'll be late on all my pickups."

"Get the fuck out of here," he said, as I peeled out, pulled out that is.

Maybe I'll keep my M-14 in the truck for a while just to save the hassle if nothing else. My biggest problem is flat tires. I've got to fix my own and prying off split rims with a sledge and a couple of pinch bars is no fun.

Paul wrote a quick note saying he'd been up in Cu Chi for a couple of weeks but was back at the 4th MI on 69 Dang Da St., so why didn't I stop down? He said he was on the night shift and so was in every day. I took off with the deuce-and-a-half for Saigon after finishing up with the wet rations one beautiful morning. I was even able to slip on an extra case of frozen steaks for the boys who were planning a barbecue this coming Sunday.

Coming up on the Newport Bridge, it occurred to me that no napalming this time along the road. It was a beautiful morning for everyone. No hitch-hikers to pick up either. 69 Dang Da was perfect in another way. I could leave the truck in the compound and not worry about it getting stripped or worse. Paul was sleeping when I found his room. Breakfast in his dining hall was something else. A late breakfast for me. The girls took orders if you could believe that and shortly presented a plate of eggs, potatoes, sausage, bacon with prepared fresh pineapple on the side. Better than any diner in the States that I'd ever been too.

"I'll tell you what, Bill, let's go water skiing. There's an old French 'relaxation' compound that the army runs on the Saigon River that keeps a couple of ski boats operating. Let's try it."

"Come on, Paul, what will they say back home if I write back saying how we've got such great skiing over here. They'd never believe it."

"You'll see. Been told it's a great spot. Good food and drinks too. Let's go."

He was right. The place was a real classy joint that still had the appearance of a French resort…with a couple of beautiful girls for waitresses. There were thatched roofs over open verandas with wood-trimmed chairs. Tennis courts covered half of one side of the grounds. Part of the shoreline was lined off for swimming, but with the brown rivers in these parts, no one was in the water. Then there were the ski boats.

An E-6 Staff Sgt. was lounging in a chaise lounge down near the boats. A selection of water skis lay on the shore.

"Hey, Sarge. What's the deal with the skis? How do we get a run?" He rather slowly turned his head our way.

"All you gotta do is fuckin ask?" he said. "This is my job."

I asked him "How the hell do you go about getting a job like this especially in Vietnam?"

"Who the hell would know that it even existed?" chimed in Paul.

We were both pretty good skiers from back home and were anxious to get going, but the sarge was in no rush to quit talking. Didn't look as if he had much company up this way, on the river.

"I was waiting around 90th Replacement for a slot to open up with my MOS when someone asked if I could run a boat. Any asshole can run a boat so against all my army experiences, I volunteered for the slot. Best gig I've ever had."

"Well, how about you giving us a tow then," said Paul and the Sarge indicated that that was fine, and asked us to find some shorts or trunks or something and get back here. I'll get the motor running."

We quickly found something to wear and joined him down at the docks. The skis were nothing fancy. Just a modernly designed all-purpose pair with a toe piece in the rear on one of them for slalom skiing. Paul jumped in the boat and I strapped on a life belt to make the first run. The boat was about a sixteen-feet fiberglass model with a sixty horsepower Evenrude outboard. It was better than any that I'd skied earlier.

"Get ready," yelled Paul as the rope tightened, and I took off on one ski. Luckily, I made it up the first try and down the river we cruised. The day was beginning to be overcast but was still plenty warm. Our side had the normal housing, some pretty shack like, but all in all rather ordinary. The off shore had no buildings but was covered with long water grass and light brush. The Sarge towed me some distance up river toward the Newport Bridge, which could be seen in the distance. He circled after a mile or so and returned to base where I was able to coast to shore without dropping in the water.

"You think you can ski like that?" I boasted to Paul. "Most assholes can" was his reply.

Paul was a two-ski man, so he waded out into the water before the Sarge towed him up and we headed west. I was in the boat watching. Suddenly, we could hear rifle fire. Then the sound of AK-47s opening up. It came from the river's edge that wasn't visibly populated.

"We'd better get the hell out of here and dock this boat fast," Sarge said as he opened the boat up faster heading for the populated shore line.

I certainly agreed, but momentarily, a Huey gunship flew directly overhead and fired off rockets into the vegetation on the far side of the river where it appeared the fire was coming from. Maybe some troopers had called in support fire for help. We looked up when the sound of another gunship was heard as rockets came in toward the off shore even lower than the last time a little behind the boat. Paul ducked. From the boat, it looked as if it might have been that close. We were quickly closing in on the dock and the last burst of rockets blew up almost on the shoreline as the gunship opened up with his mini guns all along the burning vegetation. No more choppers and the firing stopped. We were just pulling into the dock without making a circle to let Paul coast on to the beach. He was wading in dragging the skies.

"Fucking A man, that was too close for me. I ain't used to it. Even in Cu Chi so far nothing like that."

"Yea, but think, Paul, how many GIs are going to have a story like that to tell the boys when they get back in the world. No one. The absurdity of war, a fucking joke." He looked at me kind of pissed off. The Sarge was laughing.

"I don't care about the bull shit, man, I don't want to get my ass shot off, period, the story be damned."

"Come on, Paulie, don't let it get the best of you. We've lucked out again."

"You're damn right" chimed in Sarge. "You guys are lucky bastards."

"Hey, Sarge, what's your name? I'm Bill Collins, and this other yahoo who out ranks me is Paul Savage. We're friends from back home."

"Staff Sgt. Mike Kelley and I've never been waterskiing in my life. There ain't no water in New Mexico, much less ski boats. I shouldn't say no water. Me and my old man put in almost 400 acres of alfalfa on irrigated land. Six cuts, we bale hay all year. You can see why I joined the Army."

A long answer to a short question, but he was interesting. I've run into a large number of farm kids over here it seems, a number larger than the percentage of farmers in the overall US population.

We asked SGT Kelley to come up on the veranda and have a couple of beers with us. He said he shouldn't drink while on shift here but considering the last run down the river figured the hell with it.

"I've never come that close to buying the farm on this job," he said with his hand trembling just a little, "might as well be in the infantry."

"I don't think so, Sarge" points out Paul. "I've been out a few times with the 25th Infantry and that ain't no fun. The bullets come a lot closer than those rockets. Shit man, I've had people shot dead in the field with them right beside me. They could have been closer and finished us off, but they weren't. That's the difference. It they miss you the whole thing is a fucking joke. If not, well, they bag you up and send you home. Shake it off, man."

SGT. Kelly wasn't so sure, but he did indicate that he'd stick with the boats, ski boats that is, not PBRs (Patrol boat, Riverine). We lounged around the veranda of the French Compound for a spell admiring the girls working there who seemed overly friendly to SGT Kelley but what do you expect in that situation. He was with 'em full time almost. It was a short walk to the main road where we were able to find a Lambretta for the ride back to the 1st MI. Paul kept talking on about life there.

"Bill, I want to tell you about this great little girl I'm fucking on occasions. You'll never believe it, and all it cost me is the price of a room."

"How so?" I asked.

"She works up in the club. The prettiest one. Her name Ha. You've seen her up there."

"Ok, so what else. What's the deal?" He's thinking about answering.

"I'll tell you but don't laugh. For the life of me, I can't recall how we got into the topic but somehow she mentioned that she liked the feeling of a tongue in her rear end."

"You mean her ass hole?"

"Well, yea, and I said don't laugh."

"Ok, keep going."

"I kind of liked it. You know how these Vietnamese girls are so clean, washing all the time."

"I know, I see them washing the feet a dozen times a day, but that's to cool off in the hot weather. Quite frankly, I've never seen them washing 'that,' and couldn't help laughing like hell.

"Fuck you," he said starting to get pissed. "All I have to do is pay the rent for the room, which is 300p. Good deal, right."

"Great story, Paul, you almost told me exactly the same thing last time here. You've gotta get it together man." He looked startled and tried to remember.

"I had a better deal than yours, before I felt a little bit hooked up with Kim Lon. This very young girl Sau took a liking to me. I didn't bring it up, she did. She said she'd like to be in bed with me. 'I just pay mamasan 50p for bed rent.' Hell, I jumped in with her a few times. She was such a sweet girl. And I didn't have to…you know what, not that there is anything wrong with it. My deal's a lot better than yours." I said laughing.

We've got to change the subject. This conversation is getting old…or maybe sick. I was thinking too that I'd better not push my luck and get stuck in Saigon when I had to be back for the evening run with the KP girls. So, I left Paul back at his unit, jumped in the truck, and headed back up the road to Long Binh. I pulled in just in time to load up the girls and drive them for home.

"Collins, where the hell you been?" yelled Banks.

After dropping off the girls, I had stopped in at the club for some beer and to tell the boys, if they were around how the afternoon had gone down in Saigon. Most of them would never take an unauthorized military vehicle down to Saigon…especially if they were AWOL.

"I took a ride down to see my old friend Paul from home. Drove the KP truck. No problems down or back. Beats hitch hiking." I then proceeded to fill them in on the water ski trip. I wouldn't even need to exaggerate this one. It was much better than if I had made it up. Banks was drinking with Santimaw, Pacheco, and Crow along with some other regulars that I didn't hang around with. Washington was across the room with some soul brothers and gave me a smile and nod. We always got on, he and I.

Santimaw asked, "Does anyone here know how to water ski besides this bull shitter?" he laughed.

"I don't even know what it is," said Crow. There ain't no water skiing in West Virginia that I ever heard of; not where I'm from or ever been."

"You fucking hick," said Pacheco. "They water ski all over the fucking country, all over the world. But of course West Virginia ain't neither. You're probably right." This was starting to piss Crow off. He takes offense when people talk about his home country.

"No, you guys got it all wrong. The story ain't the skiing. We almost got taken out by our own helicopters. A couple of Huey gunships came blazing right over us firing rockets and miniguns into the brush on the opposite shore. Damn near hit us. Even the sergeant running the boat said he'd never seen anything like it. Shook him up."

Santimaw said, "Ok, so much for the skiing. What about the pussy if you guys were down in Saigon for the afternoon. Supposed to be fancier down that way. I bet there were some short time girls around the river where they dock the boats."

"No, just some pretty waitresses, that's all, and we didn't have time for that. It took a couple of beers to get over the rockets."

Someone started playing 'Black is Black' my favorite song for the time being. There was a beautiful girl with a great voice who sang in a Philippine band down at the 66th Supply club a few days back who belted it out for the first time for me. I can still see her singing it. But I had to go. It had been a long and complicated day. I welcomed the escape as I crawled under my mosquito net, away from the world.

A few days later, I ran into Omar at the stand in Tam Hiep. Kim wasn't around. He'd been out on an operation with some LURPs of the 199th Light Infantry Brigade.

"These guys are real fighters Collins," he said after a beer. I ordered one too. It was a hot afternoon, and I'd finished up with drys by noon.

"It be the first time I go on an operation like this. Mostly, I with normal infantry."

"So what happened? Where did you go?" I asked. He seemed reticent or something.

"Ok, man, it be a long story. They want me along to translate when they capture some NVA in Cambodia. They're sure they can, these guys. Bowie knives, long hair, they play tough, and they are tough. They pick out place just above Parrots' Beak on Cambodia border. It place where headquarters be for North and VC command, you know, the COSVN. So say the American Colonel who brief us. We have one helicopter slick that carry the six of us and one gunship for protection until they can insert us just across the border."

I'm thinking of Wilton from the 25th Infantry who was telling us of a raid his unit made into Cambodia more than two months ago. The rules of war seem flimsy indeed when independent countries' borders don't matter for a damn. Omar, however, was just getting started.

"No contact when they dropped us off. Gunships, nothing. The area at first doesn't seem to have been traveled at all for some time. We moved in a westerly direction for half an hour or so, very quietly and under cover from the thick vegetation. Darkness was setting in, so we holed up for the night right there. No guard for me for I be the interpreter. Good for Omar, right Collins?"

"Sounds great so far. How about another beer?" I ordered a two more 33s from the girl at the stand, and he continued, enjoying himself immensely.

"Early in the morning just before the sun, I can hear very quietly, some voices not so far from where we had set up for the night. I crawled slowly toward the voices and could see a group of NVA, only six or seven maybe, but have plenty guns and full NVA uniforms. They finish eating and have already got to go for the day's march. I see we cannot grab a man here and should follow them. We pack up very fast and do that all morning. We very secret. They expect nothing."

I asked him how it happened that he was sent out on this seemingly very dangerous mission. He said they needed an interpreter, and he volunteered. He said the troops on this mission were some of the good people he knew in that unit. As Omar was speaking, Kim Lon and little Hoa showed up. All they wanted was some snails. The people here ate them raw, just whacked off the small end with a large knife and sucked it out the big end. I never tried it, tho' they all swore by it. Omar was ready to continue his story.

"Then the worst happened. One our man tripped and made noise. The NVA come alert and begin firing at noise. They hit man and kill him as our patrol open up on them almost the same time. One more our man wounded, and we kill all but two of them, but they wounded but not so bad. I am able to interpret them to the LT, and they tell us that many NVA troops close by. They don't know nothing about COSVN the headquarters for all NVA and NLF operations in the south, the so-called Bamboo Pentagon. Not here in Parrots Beak."

"So, Omar, what then? You have to do something with the prisoners." He answered right off.

"I tell the LT that I believe they tell us all they know. They really just scared boys from farm country up North. The LT thinks that we have to 'di di' back to base now. Too dangerous. And that he would contact command and have them send in chopper to take us out fast as possible. He thought too much trouble to try to take prisoners with us, to just shoot them. I say no, man, these be my people, we can let them go. We cannot murder them. He say not murder, just war. Some soldier agree with him and some with me, so LT finally decide to help wounded prisoners to the helicopter and take back to headquarters for questions and torture."

"For Christ's sakes, Omar, sounds like a close call."

"Not for us, for them. NVA have close call. Helicopter come in very fast, so no problem escaping from VC territory. Other people question the NVA soldiers and torture some, but they cannot find out anything but what I tell them before. They send to POW stockade outside of Bien Hoa on old highway number one."

"I know the place, Omar. I drive right by it twice a day. They're lucky."

Omar was talked out, which was something for him. He was off looking for his girlfriend who I had not met. Kim and Hoa wanted to go back to their house, so I went along with them and felt her up a little bit, where her daughter couldn't see. Kim giggled, so I tickled her, but she slapped my hand. Not yet, she said. Maybe later, if Hoa slept. As Omar would say, "that be good for me."

CHAPTER 11

I had made a deal with Mooers. The first morning I was able finish up by 10:30 a.m. I'd take him along on a chopper provided we could catch a ride on one toward the Cambodian border where pot was supposedly available in large quantities for a cheap price. It was dirt cheap around Tam Hiep and Bien Hoa, but he was looking for a sand bag full, and he was a cheap bastard. He said he had to be in Germany because it was so much more expensive than here. Plus no combat pay in Europe. This morning was it. I stopped in at the Orderly Room to tip him off. Capt. Dewey was gone for the day with Flores, his Puerto Rican driver. Top was more or less snoozing in the back and told Carl to take off. Not much going on. We met up at the main gate, skipped out, and walked up to 11 Field Forces.

"Ok, Carl, we need a ride somewhere west near the border with Cambodia. There's a Special Forces pad that I stopped in once riding around taking pictures, but I can't remember the name. We'll just check with the gunner whenever one lands. It's odd there's none here now. It's normally busier."

"We can talk books," said Carl jokingly. "What are you reading?"

"Actually, I'm re reading *The Quiet American*; I like the mood. The intellectuals say it's the best book written about Vietnam, and it might be…but I like the mood."

"Fuck the mood, man, where's the chopper. We don't have all day." Then, right on the button, we could hear one off in the distance getting closer. He dropped off a couple of officers, and I ran over to talk with the gunner who said they were returning to An Loc and asked us to jump on. Neither of us was quite sure where An Loc was, but I knew it was generally west, northwest or something like that.

It was a clear and quiet beautiful morning, with the sun illuminating the many shades of green that covered this country. Shell holes were increasing the farther west we flew, which did not bode well for the farmers. Being one myself, I always identified with them. The Army didn't understand. We landed at a small more primitive LZ than usual some miles past Ben Cat, and jumped off. It seemed like it would be close enough, and we had to get back by six or seven. There was no guarantee that we'd even find a machine heading that way.

"Ok, wise guy, where the hell do we go from here?" asked Carl. "This is all Greek to me."

I wasn't sure either. I didn't know where the hell we were, period, but saw a GI standing off to the side of the landing pad so walked over and asked.

"You're in the fucking boondocks, that's where you are," he said. "We're an electronic listening post, mostly trying to see what we can pick up from gook radio transmissions. There is some other odd shit here but that's what I do. Tape radio traffic and have one of the interpreters here translate. We don't pick up much, but what the fuck, I'm short, six weeks. Do you think I give a damn what happens with this fucking war?"

As he didn't ask what we were doing here, I didn't volunteer anything. Just asked if there was any problem going outside the wire to look around. He confirmed there was no problem, so we headed for the gate.

"He's not that enthusiastic, is he?" asked Carl who then humorously continued with "how the hell are we supposed to win this thing with fighters like him...or for that matter fighters like us?"

"I'm not betting on winning period, the mood's not here." With that, we walked over to the gate, and as luck would have it, there was a Vietnamese soda and whatever stand not far outside. We sat down under the sheet of tin that served for an awning and ordered a beer.

"I've got a sick joke for you," said Carl. "Wanna hear it?" "Sure," I answered.

"It goes like this. I'll tell you how to win this war. You load up all the friendlies on ships and take them well off shore. Then you nuke the country... then sink the ships. So what do you think?" "I think it's sick...but funny, considering that there's more than a grain of truth to it. The lifers must love that one."

"Hey, Mamasan," I asked the woman working at the stand "Can we buy Can Sa here? We need beaucoup."

She didn't appear to understand much English but yelled out back. A young girl came over to talk with us.

"What can I do for you?" she asked in nearly perfectly accented English. "How you learn to speak English so well?" I asked her. "I am very smart," she said laughing. "I go to school and I study very hard, and then I talk GI here for long time. So you see I can learn good English."

I asked her if we could buy her a coke, and she nodded, and then I asked if she was able to sell us some Can Sa.

"You mean pot," she said, "Marijuana."

"Yes, I mean marijuana. My friend me here needs to buy a sandbag full for all of his friends back where we live. Can you do it?"

"Yes, I can do for you," she said smiling cleverly. "It will cost you twenty-five dollar MPC, You have?"

She said that it might take at least an hour for her to gather that much up, and I thought I shouldn't wait that long to look for a ride back. I had to make the night KP run by seven thirty, and we were nearly in Cambodia and had no idea how frequent the air traffic might be in this LZ. A Caribou was on approach, so it looked good for me possibly. It's amazing how little space they need to land and take off. When they parked on the ramp, I ran over and asked their destination and was told Bien Hoa.

"Help us unload and we'll drop you off there," said the crew chief. So I waved to Carl and left with them for a quick run to Bien Hoa, and as my luck was holding, a Huey was warming up near where we parked. They were talking on a load for their last stop of the day. The Huey was running medication needed at the 93rd Evac Hospital, so I'd be back home for sure, before Carl had his dope. He ought to be safe as long as he makes morning formation.

The heat was beginning to be so oppressive that I stopped in at the club for a beer. Still had over an hour to go before taking the girls home for the night. There is a young girl Hue, who had started work with the mess, who spoke very good English and who lived in Ho Nai. Her family had come down South with the partition when she was six or seven years old. She had been riding up front lately being the last one off, and we'd visit the whole time, a refreshing change from the usual relationship with females in this otherly world here.

"Collins, where you been all day?" It was Pacheco who I hadn't seen that much of lately, even tho' we lived in the same tent. He liked to sleep late and drink late in the evening, hence our missing each other.

"Hey, Pacheco, how's it going? I've been around. Actually, today Mooers and I rode a chopper off near Cambodia, so he could pick himself up a sandbag of dope. He's got a friend who's going back to his neighborhood soon and can pack it in his foot locker. For me, it was an excuse for a little adventure and help him out at the same time."

"I used to live like you in the Canal Zone. Down there I worked in the mess too, and the big business was selling food to the local hotels. Unfortunately, I was caught, hence my rank today. I'd made it to E-6; I so hated to be dropped down to E-1.

"Come on, Pacheco; you're already a Spec. 4. If I get back to PFC, I'll be lucky. I was going to bring you an egg sandwich the other morning but couldn't find you. I set aside some blue cheese specially for you." He loved food so much and was so appreciative that I'd bring him a bite from time to time."

"If you can fix me one tomorrow morning, I'll kiss you. I'll be down at the radio shop."

"If you promise not to kiss me, I'll do it."

That being said, the sound of a chopper came into earshot. It was too loud to be a Huey. Looking toward the noise, a Chinook appeared hovering over the small pad in front of Battalion Headquarters. It began lowering down and, at first glance, appeared too tight for the spot but eventually settled in.

A soldier jumped out carrying something, and the Chinook climbed straight back up and disappeared. It was Mooers. The dumb bastard gets dropped off in front of headquarters carrying a sandbag of dope. What the hell! He was heading this way, but we didn't go out not wanting to attract any more attention to him. A crowd had shown up watching the Chinook land and take off, but no one came over to question him. We met outside for the rest of the story. Fucking lucky he was.

"I've gotta hide this first," he said, so we double timed over to the hooch. "I was getting worried waiting after the girl delivered the stuff. Nothing coming or going. Finally, a Huey gunship stopped in for fuel who was on his way to Cu Chi. They let me on, and in Cu Chi, the Chinook crew chief asked me to hop in. They were going to Long Binh…he wasn't sure where. On board, I told him where I lived, and he relayed the info to the pilot. You can't see where you're going in them so when the hovered and began lowering down, I couldn't believe it. Back home, just like that. I was lucky when no one from Battalion came over asking questions. Thanks, Billy boy, it worked out just great."

"No, it was fun," I said. "A good break from the ordinary day here." I left Mooers and Pacheco who probably wanted to sample the stuff, to check the truck for the night run.

We had been force issued mutton from Australia a few days earlier. That must have been Johnson's deal to get the Aussie troops fighting in VN. I know we were paying off Marcos for the Filipinos, and they weren't fighting. They were doing aid and reconstruction work. Plus, a lot of black market dealing.

Hue came over to talk with me as I pulled up with the truck. "Collins, the women want to bring home some of the meat today. The GIs no like, and there are many left over. We no like very much either, but it food and many hungry people where we live. Can we bring home with us?"

"Sure you can, but we'd better hide it good in case the guards at the gate look through the truck." Some of them had been difficult lately, and they'd stop us on occasion just to check out the truck as an excuse to flirt with the girls.

They giggled as we found all the places in a simple deuce-and-a-half where sheep roasts could be hidden. They were rolled up in the canvas sides, packed into the tool box, and hidden under the seats and the benches in the rear. Every place but under the hood. Hue and I jumped up front and headed for the gate. We usually used the one furthest south as the first stop was Codigo. And the guards pulled us over.

"What have you got on besides the girls? We've been ordered to check all the KP trucks for stolen food." The guard wasn't that friendly, so I said nothing.

They started going over the truck and found the roasts in the tool box.

"Did you know these fucking gooks hid the meat in the truck?" He asked me.

"I'll tell you what. I don't check them at all. I know them all. They've got kids and family to feed, and if they bring home food left over that's going to be thrown in the trash, so much the better. I don't give a good fuck, period. Let 'em have the food. What the hell do you care?"

"I'll tell you why I care, he yelled. They're feeding the Viet Cong with this food. You know that as well as I do. You can't fucking fool me. All these gooks are VC, just ask 'em."

"Ok, I will." I said.

The girls were all looking out the back of the truck hoping things wouldn't get more out of hand.

"Who here is a VC?" I asked. "Come on now, speak up. We've gotta convince this guy that we're all patriotic Americans, so let's have it."

Hue talked things over with them and came forward with her statement.

"We love Americans, we no like VC." She said with a hint of a smile showing.

So I chimed in with "There is not a GI in country who'll touch this mutton and you know it. Let's face it you fuck head, you wouldn't get near this meat either. In fact, when it was served 90 percent of the GIs wouldn't even go in the mess hall it smelled so bad. You know what, this smells like shit. I don't know how those Aussies eat it."

"You're right about me," said the guard. "I wouldn't touch that shit. It makes me puke. Get the fuck out of here. I hope the VC choke to death on the god-damned stuff. And you can't fool me, I know where the food's going. I'll nail you the next time when you ain't stealing mutton."

I thought to myself "no you won't because the next time I'll not be using your gate, so you can go fuck yourself."

The girls were all laughing like hell as we pulled out, them thinking I believed that the last laugh was on the guard. Hue, who was back up front with me, was giggling as we pulled away from the gate. We had at least twenty more roasts rolled up in the canvas truck sides. So we drove on down to

Cogido for the first roast drop off. Every girl had at least one to bring home for dinner, VC or not.

The way things were going, maybe I'd be back in time to stop over in Tam Hiep and look up Kim Lon. Other girls were beginning to be less and less interesting.

It turned out that I was walking down the path to Tam Hiep just a bit before nine, hoping that Kim Lon was not sleeping, when once again I ran into Omar.

"Did you move in here?" I asked. "You're worse than me."

"I take a walk over when I feel like it," he said. "This town not be off limits to gooks." Then he laughed like hell. "Just kidding. Sick joke, man. Look for girlfriend, Lanh."

"Let's get a beer first and catch up. Been out on any operations?" I hadn't talked with him since his time with the LRRPs, so we pulled up a stool at the stand and ordered 33s."

He mentioned one that included a hot LZ insert fairly close by, between Bien Hoa and the Iron Triangle. "They sent us in with four slicks and a gunship. Too little. When the helicopter land fire so heavy that I run back the other way. Live to fight other day is my American GI motto. Three guys killed right off from helicopter I on. No good. When fighting slow down, I get back around and shoot some VC, but it not go on for a long time. Some my friends mad I lay low, but for me I have to live here and fight till the war ends. They only have to stay for one year. So maybe I think different."

"Fuck it, Omar, don't worry about it. When you look at it I think almost every GI here is trying mostly to live through that one year and get the hell out in one piece. Who wouldn't? This ain't the Second World War. It's a clusterfuck, and everyone knows it, including the big boys back in the States; they just won't admit it. They can't quite envision getting their asses kicked by a country of rice farmers on bicycles...but such is life."

Omar had quit listening and was asking the girl working the stand if she had seen Lanh. She hadn't, but there came Kim with Lanh walking up the path from the main highway. I'd have to say that Lanh was a looker who I'd seen once or twice previously at the Hope Bar. The bunch of us shot the breeze for a while; then we paired up and went our separate ways. I was hoping to end up in Kim's bed sooner than later, but she wanted to talk. There was a small bench in front of her house, a poor man's porch.

"I like to be with you more," she said as we edged closer on the seat. I tickled her taunt stomach, but she didn't take. No play, I want to talk. Soon I have to make another trip to Cambodia, see my father. He old and need money every month as I talk you before. I am thinking maybe you can go to Phnom Penh with me. We have fun. We can make love in a strange place. We can be together, my friend you. What you say?"

I thought for a minute. This would take some doing because there was no way I could skip out for three days, which is what it would take to be on the safe side. I had no passport either. Not being any kind of world traveler; it was something I'd never thought about, and it wasn't needed when "touring" with the army. At least not so far.

"If I did try, Kim, how would I get across the border and, possibly more difficult, how would I get back into Vietnam on the ride home. Is Hoa coming with us?"

"No can do this time. She love her grandpa, but she stay with mamasan. I will find how to get you across the border and back to this side. Not sure now but can do."

We left it at that and snuggled a bit and on coaxing more, she mentioned "I have blood. No make love tonight."

"We can kiss then, beaucoup." We tickled and kissed till dusk like the kids we were. The stars were out in full, like the night sky back on the farm, as I walked back toward the beginning of the Tam Hiep trail.

Not a week later, when I still hadn't figured out how to attempt a trip to Cambodia with Kim, the problem was solved for me. It was a dark quiet morning while I was driving along a dirt road along the Long Binh perimeter when a siren and flashing lights appeared behind me. I pulled over and waited. An MP shortly appeared at my window and said that I was speeding, forty in a twenty-five zone. I couldn't believe it. A speeding ticket in Vietnam while driving along an absolutely empty dirt road at four thirty in the morning. Fuck me, or fuck me dead as Sandy would say.

The MP said "you're getting a ticket. You know the speed limit here."

I told him "I did like hell. I didn't know they had speed limits here."

He said, "you drunk or something; there's a sign right behind you."

I replied, "who cares, give me the ticket," thinking I hope this guy doesn't screw up my job.

The way things were going, I'd given up on finding something more involved with the war. The so-called operations in the Ammo Dump would have to suffice. I'd checked in with Mr. Vann a couple of times, and it was apparent nothing was going to materialize in that office either. As far as 1049s went, I'd given up on them too. The word from the Orderly Room was that if a soldier couldn't find a slot ahead of time in the company he wanted the transfer into, and if he didn't have an officer or NCO in that company speaking for him, a transfer wouldn't take place; period. And I'd lost interest in being a door gunner because I wasn't interested in having to shoot people. Earlier I hadn't thought about it that much, just that it'd be a great escape up in a chopper and, quite frankly, exciting. For now, Kim Lon and Tam Hiep were more than enough, plus the occasional escape to Saigon to see Paul.

Two days later, I ran into Carl and he told me the Capt. was looking for me. I'd better stop in and see what he wanted. Capt. Dewey said, "I'm yanking your license, Collins. You have trouble, you are trouble at times, but you've got to play by the rules here. That's the army, and I'm the army."

I went through the whole deal with him, dirt road, four thirty in the morning, the whole deal but he had made up his mind. So I tried the job deal. I was doing a lot for these birds. One man picked up rations for 500, picked up the girls early morning, and returned them late at night. I had to make out that it was really a hard job. "I know all that," said Capt. Dewey "so I'm not taking you off the job. I'll give you a driver. I think Maldanado would work out for you. He's good friends with my driver Flores."

I never expected this but shut my mouth and went along thinking that the joke was on him. Here I am the lowest ranking GI in the company with my own deuce-and-a-half, and now a SP 4 driver. Captain Dewey, the highest-ranking man in the company, only has a jeep along with his SP 4 driver. It'll be interesting to see where this goes.

It went better than expected, much better. I was acquainted with Maldonado and came to know him well in quick measure. Not a brilliant guy but very good hearted and capable as long as I dragged him out of bed in the morning. He couldn't get up worth a damn.

"Come on, Collins, you know I wake up slow. I'm from Puerto Rico." This being his favorite saying as he came around.

"Maldi," that's what I called him, "if they stop me without you driving, I'll lose this spot and that can't happen. Besides you can keep this for yourself after I leave, and you'll never find a better job in the green machine, not in this world."

He told me that this was a much better gig than his buddy Flores had who drove for the CO. Apparently, he was either driving with him or hanging around the Orderly Room waiting to do so. Never had any free time, and none at all with a vehicle. It did take a while for Maldonado to learn the ropes. He had been one of those guys who hardly ever left the base camp and consequently wasn't familiar with the area streets and highways. It wasn't long before we were both tested.

The cooks informed us that there was to be a large party for the Battalion in the mess hall this coming Saturday evening. The rumor was that a number of White girls were to be in attendance. Also, a number of officers were to attend, not low-ranking EM like us.

"You get it," said Maldonado. "Round-eye pussy only for the officers; they're too good for the local girls. No gooks for them."

"Well, what did you expect?" I asked, "you know the litany 'The only good gook is a dead gook', 'If it's dead it's VC', 'Kill 'em all and let God sort them out.' There's no end to it. These fuckers will never come around. The problem we are going to have is that the KP girls want to stay late just so they can see what these 'super women' look like. They've never known any...probably never seen one."

"I don't know Collins," you'd better stay away from that. We'll run the girls home and forget about it. Just explain to them."

I didn't want to "just explain" for I'd already told Hue that we could go home an hour or so later that night figuring if a problem did arise it wouldn't matter much any way. We'd just leave. On the way home that night, I was explaining it all to Hue.

"What you mean, Collins, we no can watch party. We all bring good clothes and change so look nice like all American girls."

"Don't worry, Hue, we'll do it." I didn't have the heart to say no.

Saturday night came to be. The plan was after the dining area had been super cleaned, they'd change clothes in the dishwashing area and just watch the goings on from the doorway. We'd not intrude at all, including myself and Maldi since we weren't invited either. However, each of us had a right to be there; it was our duty station after all.

Maldonado wasn't much of a drinker. I was and had a few beers from the ice barrel "without being invited." There was plenty there. The dining area was filling up. The Colonel was walking around proud as hell with a pretty WAC, round eyed and white, as you'd expect. Lesser officers including Captain Dewey were doing their best trying to make up with the other girls. The funny thing was most of them were enlisted like Maldi and me. There were hardly enough women army officers in country to make a dent. So the big boys had to lower themselves, but not so low as to take up with a "Vietnamese." Not that man, we're better than that. If they only knew. The girls had gathered around the gate dressed in their finery all agog watching the going ons. As far as they were concerned, the round-eyed girls were Hollywood, for even in the jungle and shanty towns of war-torn Vietnam, that dream prevailed. And then the 1st Sgt. We were all in the washing area not affecting the party at all.

"What the fuck these gooks doing here?" he bellowed. "Get their asses home, Collins, you should know better than this."

I'd had enough beer to get vocally pissed off at this rude fuckhead and yelled right back, "They work here, doncha know?"

"They ain't fucking working now. Get them the hell home before the Colonel or some other officer notices and they get my ass."

"Why, they work here. Why would they say anything? There's nothing out of order."

Then he really lit into me. "You're drunk, you fucking ass hole, you've always been nothing but trouble and you can't drive either. I'll find a driver."

"I've got a driver right here, Maldonado. We'll take them home. Go back to your round-eyed party." From his look, I knew that I'd better watch my ass in the near future.

I might be drunk but was ashamed of being associated with the 1st Sgt; he embarrassed the girls so. It pissed me off, man. It was the same old thing.

They're just gooks, they don't know the difference; they don't have feelings like us, and they don't value life like we do; it goes on and on. I told them I was sorry, but we had to go. They took it in stride. They're used to anything, most of them believing half the time we bomb and shoot them just for the fuck of it and run them over on the highway. We're a great bunch out saving the world for democracy.

We were driving down toward Codigo for the first stop. Hue rode in the back with the other girls. After thinking about it, she had no use for us. I'd tried to explain we'd done all we could. "I'll tell you what, Maldonado, somehow I've got to straighten things out with the 1st Sgt. Apologize or something. Maybe bring him some specialty food from the ration point. Something….or he'll be fucking over me."

"Don't worry, I'll have Flores talk to the Capt. They're getting to be almost friends. I mean he's an officer, and Flores is from Puerto Rico so that's something."

"The thing is I'm hoping to get a pass or some kind of authority to look up my two cousins who are in I Corps. One's a Sgt 1st class in the 1st Cav. in Camp Evans just above Hue where he is organizing a medical clinic before the division moves in full force The other is working as a farm advisor with IVS. He ran a dairy farm for years near our home place."

"What the fuck's IVS?" asked Maldonado.

"International Voluntary Services. It's like the Peace Corps, but the word is it's CIA backed but that doesn't matter. He does something with the farmers in that area."

"Well," said Maldonado, "from the news on the bombing and spraying up by the DMZ, he's probably just trying to get 'em fed. It's full of craters, and you can't grow shit on land sprayed with herbicides. I'm enough of a farmer to know that."

We finished up late, but I stopped in at the club to see if anyone was still there. Most of the boys were. Mooers, Banks, Pacheco, other faces I couldn't put a name to. They were asking how the party went. How did the round-eyed pussy look? Typical GI questions.

"Some looked good, some looked extra good, just like girls everywhere. Me, I've got no problem with the locals."

"Yea, well, watch it, Collins," said Banks, "some of the lifers got you pegged as a gook lover. And I might add, we've already heard about you yelling at the 1st Sgt about the girls from the mess hall. That ain't gonna go down well. You'd better watch your ass."

"Don't worry, Carl here is going to cover my ass in the orderly room, right Mooers?"

"I'll try, you dumb fuck, but that guy is a hard ass. You usually keep a tight lip. What the hell happened?"

"He was being a prick, and I had too much beer, shit man, it happens. It's not the end of the world."

"If you're lucky," said Mooers.

That talk finally ended, and after a few more beers, we all headed off to our mosquito nets.

Days later. I was over at Kim Lon's little house in Tam Hiep. I loved being under her mosquito net beside or under or over her naked body. It was like living in a small piece of heaven. Maybe considering the heat the two of us generated and the outside temperature, it was like a small part of hell. Either way was alright by me. She kept talking about making a trip with her to Cambodia.

"You know, Collins," she began almost giggling, "it very hot this time of year in Cambodia, hotter than here. Maybe there we can make more hot."

A lot more hot sounded great, but this talk of sneaking a trip to Cambodia was wearing me down, but I was beginning to see how I could make it work. Possibly. First, I was hoping that Captain Dewey would approve a trip up country to see my two cousins. In-country three-day passes weren't that common, mainly because there was no great need for them. They were issued for in-country R&Rs and visits with relatives in the service who were stationed in another more distant part of the country. That fit me perfectly. All would be legal if the 1st Sgt didn't fuck it up.

"Ok, Kim, let's make it more hot." We were becoming touchingly familiar with each other's nakedness so hot was easier, a dreamlike ecstasy. I left in the very early morning to arrive in time for the KP run thinking a side trip to Cambodia with her could be very interesting.

CHAPTER 12

"HERE'S your pass, Collins. You'll have to get out to Tan Son Nhut and find your own transport. Be back on time, you hear."

"Got it, Captain, thanks again." It turned out that the 1st Sgt withheld any negativity toward me. He probably thought it best to let it go as did I. I mean hell, I did get the work done for them without any headaches normally, so why not? I didn't mention my cousin Emerson Fitz, the former farmer who was working with IVS in the Da Nang area. I wasn't sure how they'd view a pass to visit with a civilian. Emerson's brother, Charlie the Sgt. 1st Class was perfect, an all-army rendezvous. I'd look up Emerson in Da Nang, and we'd make it up to Camp Evans one way or another hoping that Charlie was there and not out in the field. The 1st Cavalry Division (Airmobile) was not a static outfit.

I figured to stop first at II Field Forces and catch a quick ride to Ton Son Nhut. I pulled in at Kim Lon's hooch on the way to the main gate to give her a hidden kiss and say good bye.

"You no get hurt, my friend Collins," she said. "I need you."

With those reassuring words I walked quickly toward the gate carrying a small hand bag up to the helipad. It was not yet 7:00 a.m., and choppers were coming and going, dropping off various hotshots for the day's work. In short order, I was landing in Saigon. The load master there advised catching an Air Vietnam flight to Na Trang or Cam Ranh Bay where it should be easy to hop the rest of the way to Da Nang on choppers. I preferred the low road to see what was happening in the country up that way.

Air Vietnam had some sort of arrangement with Continental Air to provide operational support in the theatre so that military personnel theoretically would have quick access to transport…and this time I had papers. Within half an hour, I was in the air heading for Nha Trang in an old Vietnam Airlines DC-3. I was the only US military on board but so far so good. No one asked to see my pass so far either. This plane did have chickens though; they had their feet tied, which might have been a good thing as the old Mamasans jabbered away.

The bomb craters had grown in numbers since my last chopper ride east of Bien Hoa. We soon passed into new territory for me, but the bomb craters kept appearing as we flew along with the coast on the right. It looks like a fairly low altitude flight, beautiful coastline on the right and bomb craters with choppers and bombers doing their thing on the left. I was sitting next to an ARVN Lieutenant who spoke a bit of English and began talking.

"Where you go? Many times I take this plane between Nha Trang and Saigon but never see many American GIs. My family in Saigon so I come see them when I can."

"What kind of unit are you in?" I asked him. "Do you work with the Americans in Nha Trang?"

"Sometimes we do operations together, but I no like. They think they know it all. We know nothing. I no like that." It looked like he was beginning to get angry.

I changed the subject. "Is this a VC area we are flying over now?" I asked him.

His reply was right up front. "All Vietnam country VC area, but not cities. Countryside VC. Cities some. Who can know?"

I switched off to the weather. It seemed like a safe topic. "Americans put something in clouds to make rain in dry season. Not good. Poison. We no like."

OK, we can perhaps talk about the beautiful view on the right of the plane along the coast. The beaches that stretched forever in each direction were quite breathtaking. He doesn't seem interested in that and switches conversation to the ARVN soldier on his other side. The rest of the flight proved to be uneventful, which can be a good thing in most any part of Vietnam. Approach and landing at the Nha Trang airfield also proved "uneventful."

Not being able to find any fixed wing transport further north, I tried the helicopter landing area nearby and was soon successful. A warrant officer named Rob Tallon helped me out. He was flying a slick up as far as Da Nang with stops at Quang Ngai and Chu Lai.

"Mostly I'm dropping off paperwork on my proscribed stops," said Tallon. "You never know who else might jump on, but I'll hook you up with a helmet with intercom so we can shoot the shit along the run. You haven't been up this way before, have you?"

"Hell no. Mostly been stuck in the area of III Corps from Saigon / Bien Hoa to the Cambodian border. This is turning into a great trip. I'm lucky to run into you."

"Let's hope so," he said, "we don't wanna get shot down giving you a tour. What the fuck are you doing? Got work up that way or something?"

"No, no, I scored a pass to go look into a couple of cousins up in Da Nang and Camp Evans with the 1st Cav. Seemed like a good excuse to take a trip and look over the country."

Tallon pointed to a slick over near a fuel bladder and said jump in behind the left seat. Said that the helmet there would work for me, that it was already plugged in and operable. Lucky for me so far. The co-pilot and gunners jumped on board, and in short order, we were airborne. Once again, beautiful countryside marred by bombs on the left with that magnificent coastline on the right.

The farther north we flew, the greater the destruction. I'd tried out the intercom, which worked well.

"Hey, Tallon, what's been going on up this way? Half the houses along this route are burned."

"That's the war from here at least to Chu Lai. The feeling is that the VC are so entrenched that the only way to get them is to kill and burn anything in sight. It's pretty tough. That's why I prefer this duty. Most of the time, I fly a gunship. I'll tell you more when we get on the ground in Quang Ngai."

All I could think is that by now everyone that lived up this way was certainly VC, if for nothing else just for survival. I know they dropped leaflets warning people that bombing was imminent, but where the hell would you go? Most locals lived their lives as locals. All their friends and relatives lived in close proximity. There would be nowhere to go.

Omar had told me he was on an opps of some kind or relief interpreter north of Nha Trang. I forget the unit. But he mentioned that it was a hell of a lot worse to survive up here if you were a local farmer. Too much firepower.

I could see F-4s and Huey gunships near the foothills inland as we approached Quang Ngai. They were too far in the distance to make out what they were bombing and strafing, but it certainly didn't bode well for the people living up that way. Kim's lucky she lives in Tam Hiep. This place looks like hell for the local farmers. Rob had to fuel the chopper after landing and wait till his man picked up the currier pack.

"Like I was telling you, Collins, there's a lot of talk about warning people of upcoming operations where they will be bombed if they don't get out, but the refugees in these two provinces number in the hundred thousand. We've got relocation camps, as do some Vietnamese organizations, but in no way can all the people be taken care of. I hate to admit it, but we don't give a damn really. It's easier to just say they're all VC. What else can you do? We're supposed to win the war and that's done with body counts."

"We, I hate to say it, Tallon, but it looks to me like the way to lose the war is to keep this up. I always tell the guys down my way who don't get first-hand knowledge of this kind of destruction that the fuckheads running this war never could understand 'that if you bomb and burn a man's house, kill his wife and kids, poison his fields, kill his water buffalo, it's very unlikely that he is going to be your friend'. Realistically, he and his kin are going to be your enemy for generations."

"Well, maybe," said Tallon. "I suppose, but we follow orders. A couple of more months, I'll be out of here for good, and none too soon. Fucking A man."

He continues "It's getting sicker here too. A gunship pilot was talking the other day about KBAs. That's Killed By Air, our lingo for body counts. He was saying that if he hits a pregnant woman, it counts for two KBA. Sick man, think about it."

"Enough of that shit, man," I said. "Let's get going."

"We're off," said Tallon. "Almost a touch and go to drop off a packet at Chu Lai, then di di into Da Nang."

As we were flying along toward Chu Lai, FACs. fighter bombers and all types of Hueys were visible doing their things throughout the county side.

It resembled a bad movie. A remarkable beautiful country being systemically destroyed. Where the fuck are the brains. On the approach to the base at Chu Lai, we took a couple of rounds of small arms fire but luckily no one was hit, and more importantly, no hydraulic lines were hit. That might finish us all.

I met a guy at the field in Chu Lai waiting for a ride to Phu Cat, a Dr. David Forrest who was teaching for the University of Maryland.

"You've never heard of us?" he asked. I hadn't actually and didn't recall their being any representation from that school in Long Binh.

"I teach History for them," he said. "It's a good program. You can get your college degree while shooting the gooks. Just kidding. I'm very aware that that's more than a sick joke. It's sick, period. This place will do that to you. But we do have a great program for GIs who want to get on in the world."

I told him that maybe I should look into that but knew that I wouldn't. For the time being, I was getting my education in Tam Hiep from the girl Kim Lon. Anything else could wait, first things first. I said farewell to Dave as Tallon approached, and we loaded up on the Huey for the run to Da Nang. The scorched earth policy followed us all the way.

"Good knowing you, Collins," said Tallon after he'd dropped off his paper work. "I'm going on to Phu Bai for the night and then off tomorrow wherever they send me. "Good Luck."

I thanked him profusely and then wandered off thinking how the hell I'm going to find my cousin Emerson. After asking around someone mentioned that there might be an IVS office down near the US Consulate on Bach Dang St. along the river. I jumped on a motorbike outside the airfield and off we went. Da Nang resembled Bien Hoa to a great extent. Perhaps all Vietnamese towns looked the same to a GI from the farm. Who could tell?

It was getting dark as we pulled up to the Consulate. I asked the guard outside about the IVS office, and he pointed up the street. I walked a bit and there it was, a bit shabby for a US Government outfit I thought as I walked through the door, and there he was.

"Bill, where the fuck did you show up from? How did you find me?" said Emerson as he walked over and gave me a hug. We lived on neighboring farms back home.

"It's great to see you, Em. You wouldn't believe the trip up here. It's hundreds of miles to where I'm at near Bien Hoa. Christ, you look good. Must be you found some nice pussy."

"Yea, well, first my secretary, Chi. You'll meet her tomorrow. We've got a little friendship going on, if you get my drift. It sure as hell beats beating off with bag balm."

We both laughed like hell at that one. He showed me around and talked of various projects he'd been working on, but as I had imagined he spent most of his time trying to help the refugees from the bombing with housing and food.

"You be surprised, but I've had the best of luck working with a Vietnamese outfit sponsored by the Cao Dai sect, a branch of Buddhism. The military are so fucked up they're about worthless. But let's get down to a bar and forget about all that for a time. I'm thinking of the Bamboo. This chick Yim runs it. You'll love her. Young and beautiful."

Between the fishing boats and the US Navy, the piers along the shoreline of the Han River were crowded. Near the northern end of Bach Dang St. was the Bamboo tucked in with some shacks along the small part of the shoreline that wasn't lined with boats. The Bamboo was crowded, mostly with GIs, though there were a few civilians and as usual for Vietnam, a number of pretty bar girls.

"You'll find that most of the girls here don't speak much English," said Emerson. "They work for tips only and the chance to better their English. Always working, the Vietnamese. I always imagine how this country would be if we weren't over here blowing it up."

"Well, at least it ain't communist." I said jokingly. "That's what matters to the Americans."

"For sure. Bill, this is Yim. She the boss here." A strikingly pretty girl, very young, was sitting across the bar from us.

"How are you, Bill," said Yim. "Glad to meet you."

"And I am certainly glad to meet you too, Yim" said I. Then for a bit we engaged in the usual banter between GI and Bar Girl. Emerson of course did not consider himself a GI at all, in no way. He'd always been independent back home.

"Those fuckers can't ever let go of the gook syndrome, which is what I call it" he said. "They can't just shut the fuck up. It's embarrassing for us all, including the Vietnamese. They don't call us White Trash in most cases. Of course, they wouldn't be much off if they did half the time."

Emerson had been over here longer than I had, though we had both left the farms at the same time. Somehow, he had gotten himself hooked up with IVS. We had a few beers. I checked out the girls, all of whom knew Em.

"So is IVS a CIA operation?" I asked him. "You hear it all the time, but usually from people who don't know what they're talking about. Hey, you know I met John Paul Vann down in Bien Hoa. He run's USAID there. You ever met him."

"No, I haven't, no way…but I've heard of him. He's got a little baggage, that guy, but apparently, he's doing a hell of job down your way. You know USAID is not uninvolved with the CIA. It's all the US Government, one way or the other."

We eventually got off the topic of our lives here in Vietnam and caught up on the gossip from home, which is the same all over the world, "who's fucking whom." After that we got down to business figuring out how we'd get up to see his brother "Babe," real name Charles Fitzpatrick. Babe had been in the army for at least ten years; he was a sergeant 1st class, a medic and from a card he had sent me, setting up a clinic at Camp Evans ahead of the entire 1st Cav. Division that was expected sometime in the near future.

"We could always try to catch a chopper up there, or at least to Phu Bai, but I'd kind of like to drive. I've been using an old Renault, the same model that is used in Saigon for taxi cabs, I'm sure you're familiar with it."

"Well, is that road open? You're got to drive over the Hai Van Pass, which looks wide open to any yahoo with a gun. After that it looks good, but you know the territory, Em, I don't but I'd just as soon not get my ass shot off at this point."

"You think I do," said Emerson. "I've recently driven to a refugee encampment just beyond Hue once or twice with no problem, so let's give it a try. There's lots of military along that route during the day, so I'm not worried. Only daylight driving though; the VC own this countryside after dark, just like in the rest of the country."

"What do you think about that?" I asked. "The Brass reads it differently."

"You flew over the countryside from Nha Trang to Da Nang at a fairly low altitude I presume. Do you think anyone left in the farm country along that route could possibly side with the Americans or the ARVN after they've destroyed nearly all the land and the houses? I work in these refugee camps to a certain extent. There ain't no love lost there for either. Fuck it man, it ain't logical, but the dumb fucks can't figure it out apparently. They love bombing."

"Hey, Em, man, you don't have to convince me. I'm with you. Back at the Company, they call me the 'gook lover.' I might add that most of the locals that I know are pretty girls, so why not love them."

"Yim, one more round of beer please." I asked. "Alright, Em, let's drive in your car. I'll think I'm back in Saigon, though I've never actually used their taxis. Just the cyclos."

We downed the beer and walked back to his office. Once inside, we downed half a bottle of good cognac someone had left him. Sure as hell hit the spot. The back room where he slept was even less presentable than the front office. Two or three cots on a cement floor with a couple of blankets. No mosquito nets, and you could hear the rats scurrying around in the middle of the night.

Bright and early the next morning, the old Renault was churning up the first slope of Hai Van Pass, which already was breathtakingly beautiful. The sun was climbing over the horizon of the South China Sea and the traffic thus far was light. Emerson pointed out a leper colony, which lay along the shore of the ocean and which could be reached only by boat from the Da Nang port. Occasionally, he stopped by with clothing and other treats to these people who had to manage by themselves. Apparently, the thinking about lepers in these parts was still "old testament." They were feared by all.

Halfway up, we ran into heavy truck traffic and were barely crawling along. Emerson thought we'd lose half an hour or so but were getting along as he had expected. There was a great view up and down the country and out into the sea from the top, which still had operational pill boxes that the French had built during the 1st Indo China war. Without close inspection, they appeared to be manned by ARVN troops. Who knew about the night, for I'd read *The Quiet American* a couple of times?

Marine Corps traffic was picking up heavily from the pass to Phu Bai. It seemed odd to me that the Cav was setting up above Hue when the Marine Corps ran this war zone, I Corps. Somebody must know more than this private. Emerson decided to pull in at the main gate to the airfield to check on the situation above Hue if there was anything going on.

"I just had a jeep full of grunts pull in here from Camp Evans, and they seemed to think things were calm throughout that route. I'd say go for it. Ain't heard nothing else," said the guard.

The traffic picked up through Hue with the bridge by the Citadel nearly choked off, but patience won out eventually, and we were cruising along north once more. Emerson wanted to stop in at a refugee camp he'd checked out earlier in the month three or four kliks north, which we arrived at momentarily. It sure as hell didn't look like much. More like a shanty town that couldn't have had much in the way of services. We pulled over and stopped at a tent at the entrance driveway, which appeared to be the headquarters. Emerson stuck his head inside, and finally, a girl, a pretty girl, came out. She said her name was Huong and that she was the only one here now.

"I boss number one," she said laughing in good English. "What are you guys looking for?"

Emerson explained that he'd been working here earlier with a Mr. Hai and wondered where he might be.

"He dead," said Huong. "Mr. Hai was down in the countryside west of Chu Lai. Airplane come and drop bombs and he die with most of the village. We miss him here but now I am boss."

"That's terrible," said Emerson to the girl. "He was a good man who made things work here, which is difficult as I imagine you know. How's it going now?"

"We have about like before, but you can see too many people without house and food. Same old problem."

"I go back to Da Nang tonight or tomorrow and will see if I can find some help for you. Good luck till then, Huong. I will be back."

We climbed back into the Renault heading north where a left turn off three or four kliks ahead should take us to Camp Evan.

"All l can tell you, Bill, is that you fuckers are not fixing this country. Keep at it, and there won't be one."

I shrugged and said nothing. Repeating my routine mantra won't do much. We followed the railroad track along Highway 1 and turned left at the cemetery, which was on the ocean side of the tracks. This was the beginnings of Camp Evans, headquarters of the 1st Cavalry Division (airmobile). SGT 1st Class Charles "Babe" Fitzpatrick was the NCO in charge of the medical clinic for the 7th of the 7th, Gerry Owen, Custer's unit, the most legendary regiment in the US Army. Babe was a drinker. The private at the gate sent us directly to the medical tent. Babe was sitting at his desk inside with the sun shining through the tent flap enjoying a late morning bracer. Hell, Ten High bourbon could be had for a buck eighty in any PX.

He rushed over and gave Emerson a hug saying, "Where the hell did you find our cousin? He's supposed to be winning the war in Saigon. That's what I heard."

We shook hands, laughed and enjoyed an Irish coffee all around. Babe loved having the company. Apparently, Emerson hadn't been up to see him either, not knowing he was this close till I let him know. It's easy to get stuck in your own rut in this man's army. First, Emerson had to go over the same gossip from last evening for Babe's benefit. He had a wife and a couple of kids back home so missed out on the risqué gossip that Emerson picked up from the "stables" back on the farm.

"When I was back in An Khe, they were short medics on a dust off where we were having to extract a company with heavy casualties who had been dropped into a hot LZ that positively erupted into a gigantic firefight. They had no protection until gunships arrived to lay down some rockets and force the NVA back with miniguns. I went in with them to patch up the most badly shot up so they wouldn't bleed out returning to triage. Damn near died. Got grazed three times but hardly bled. They're not dishing out a purple heart for that. Not in this unit. I know Bill, down your way they'd probably stick on a Bronze Star along with the Purple Heart for those wounds and that kind of bravery."

"Yea, they might" I said, "but so far I've been luckier than anyone could hope for…and I hope it stays that way. I don't need medals."

"Nor do I." Babe said, "but you've gotta show a hell of a lot more than that to pick up a medal in the Cav. We're a tough bunch of bastards."

"No doubt," said Emerson. "I could get my ass shot off by either side, and no one with IVS or the government would remember my name. We are the unknown cogs operating alongside the 'Green Machine' you guys work with. I don't give a damn because the poor bastards that live here deserve some help so I do what I can."

"I admire all the people like you," I said, "more than the regulars." When it's all said and done, you guys are going to get nothing but your measly paycheck. At least we got the VA."

"You never know, I might get myself a wife out of this," said Emerson. "Chi's a good girl."

"I thought she was just a friendly fuck," I said, "what's going on?"

"Nothing any of you birds need to know. Later maybe. She and I are private. Let it go."

Enough said on that. I had to get back to Long Binh by tomorrow evening and figured it'd be best to make it back to Da Nang by dark. Emerson agreed. He had no interest driving through the pass after sunset, no way. We bade Babe farewell and drove on back through Hue almost reaching Phu Bai before being stuck in traffic. It'll be a push at this rate to make the "Bamboo" by dark.

"I'll buy the beer tonight," I told Emerson as we took over some bar stools. We had indeed made it through the pass before darkness had set in, but it was pitch black as we ordered some 33s from Yim. Lucky again.

"We don't want to be that late tonight," said Emerson. "There's a good chance you can catch a ride back early on a DC 3 either to Saigon or possibly right into Bien Hoa Airfield. There should be a couple of milk runs taking off early. You know, daylight."

I was considering that if I could make it back by tomorrow evening, I'd head over to Tam Hiep and spend the night with Kim Lon. I was missing her. I was hooked on her. I didn't want to go home. I'd leave her place early enough to make the morning KP run with Maldonado and then check in at the orderly room. Good cover if it all worked out.

"Where are you from, Yim?" I asked as she brought over the 33s. "Are you a city girl or a country girl?"

"My family had a pepper farm in Tra My, but we no have now. Bombs. All plants destroyed so now just garden and chickens and one pig. I send home money from this bar. When war over we can plant more pepper but now no way. We hope."

"You know what, Emerson, that story's getting old. Do you think the old bastards running the military will ever leave here? They'll never win, I know that. I'd bet the farm on it. But I hope I don't 'buy the farm' if you get my drift."

"Where the hell did that saying come from?" he asked me. "Buy the farm."

"The first World War, an earlier 'big one'. Just ask the old lifers. The death benefit paid in that war was ordinarily about enough to pay off the mortgage on the farm. Everyone lived on a farm then, so the saying worked. Clever, right?"

"I guess so. One more beer, and we're turning in. Man, I'm tired."

I agreed, so we drank up and said out good byes to Yim and walked back down Bach Dang Street to Em's office. I didn't want to miss the plane in the morning, or miss meeting Chi.

We were awakened by the ebullient Chi. It was easy to see why Emerson was taken by this charming and beautiful young woman. She had coffee made, so after dressing and washing it down, I said good bye after hardly meeting her and with Emerson drove off to the airfield.

"If we can't get you on a flight there, we'll try the Marble Mountain field over in the Marine compound on China Beach. Smaller craft use the field frequently as well as C-47s. One thing about you military people, you don't lack for aircraft."

No doubt about that. The Da Nang field like Saigon and Bien Hoa contained every type or aircraft in the Air Force inventory. A U-2 was taking off as we pulled into the terminal. We checked around for an hour or so with no luck. One C-47 had left earlier for Saigon, but nothing else was expected till at least afternoon. Helicopters were available one hop at a time for however long it might take, but Emerson thought it best to head over to Marble Mountain and return here later if nothing was available.

After another hour of checking flights, I found myself in an Air America Turo Porter flying direct to Saigon. Air America is a CIA operation, but they had no opposition to my boarding for the flight down. I thanked Emerson for all his help, for all of us were glad to see each other. A rather unusual connection from my experience with the Army here in VN.

The pilot flew on a course more inland than the Huey on the way north, which only exposed more destruction of the same. Very few buildings left of any kind with most of the landscape covered with bomb craters. The foothills showed evidence of herbicide sprays like those used around the outskirts of the Ammo Dump. Brown burned off brush. I'd had grunts tell me that in the mountains where spraying had been applied and killed all the trees, the vegetation that grew back was twice as hard to navigate than the original. So you had to wonder what's the point. Whatever.

It looked as if we'd make Saigon early afternoon, and I was thinking I'd hitch hike up to Long Bien and stop to see Paul at 4th MI Battalion on the road north. He'd probably have more stories about bedding down Hanh, the girl who worked in his club. He so dearly loved to talk, especially on girls and sex.

The Porter made quick work of the trip down and after an uneventful flight and landing I was able to catch a ride to Dong Da St and began walking down to Paul's company. Once again, he was in.

"Bill, where the hell did you come from? He asked as I walked into his room.

"You won't believe this, Paulie, but the CO gave me a pass to travel to Da Nang to look up my cousin Charile Fitzpatrick, Babe, you know him. His brother Emerson is working in Da Nang with an aid outfit, IVS, so I spent time with them both." It took a while to fill him in on the trip and catch up on our happenings since we'd last seen each other. We spent at least an hour in his club drinking beer.

I started thinking about Linh, from the Gala bar. "You been downtown lately?" I asked. "The Kangaroo, or the Gala?"

"Checked in at the Gala but no Linh. The girl on the bar didn't know what had happened to her. She'd not been in for at least a couple of weeks. The Kangaroo was as per. Sandy, Tot, and Kanh with a mix or GIs from the locals to Grunts who'd managed to get to Saigon on one pretext or another. Sandy hadn't seen Flynn but thought he might have gone to Cambodia, or maybe Israel. He wasn't sure. Otherwise pretty quiet."

"I'll try to get down sometime next week and maybe we can make the run. First, I've got to get back on track in the company. Don't want to take any chances on screwing up my job there, it's working out so well."

"I'm doing damn near as well as myself," said Paul, "if we can keep it up till we get the hell out of here."

"That's all we can do," I said, "Keep trying. I've got to get going. I want to check in with my faithful driver Maldonado and Carl in the Orderly Room and then skip out to Tam Hiep if the coast looks clear."

Paul walked me to the front gate and once again I started hoofing north. After a mile or so, a jeep stopped, and I hopped in. A Spec 4 was driving and said his destination was Thu Duc.

"I think I'll take the back road," said the driver. "You know that route?"

"Sure." I said. "Last time I was on it and ran into the middle of an operation run by ARVN troops. No Americans around. Luckily an interpreter from the 199th was with them, and he helped me out. I'll tell you, it did worry me, but in the end, no problem."

"Ah, hell, I take it from time to time. It's like a back road back home. I'm off a farm in Iowa, how about you?"

"Off a farm in NY State. You milk cows?" I asked him.

"Doesn't everyone?" he said laughing. "I've met more fucking cow milkers in this man's army than I ever did back home. Didn't anyone else get drafted?"

We talked about farming for the rest of the run. It was fun. In Thu Duc, he dropped me near the main highway. Right off, a deuce-and-a-half stopped and gave me a ride back to the company. This was great, Da Nang and back home with no trouble at all. Inside I was thinking this was a warmup for a clandestine trip to Cambodia with Kim Lon. Might as well push it to the limit. After all, what are they going to do "send me to Vietnam.

They were all at the club. I stopped in after meeting up with Maldonado at the mess hall. He was just pulling out with the girls, and I let him know I'd be on the morning run with him. He'd had no problems taking care of things while I was gone, which bode well for Cambodia.

"Collins, you cocksucker, I was just telling these guys you'd never make it back on time. The Captain was ready nail you too if you were late. I was set to cover though."

"Good man, Carl, but you knew I'd make it. All my connections both ways were so agreeable you'd never believe it. Not one ugly word. Almost made me believe in the Army…if it weren't for the razed country up there." I'll let it go with that. The first thing you know, one of these clowns will start with the "gook lover" shit.

Banks and Santimaw were sitting off to the side talking. "What's with you two?" I asked. "Anything go down over the weekend?" "Later," said Banks.

"Hey, Collins, my man," said Pacheco cracking a smile, "I could use an egg sandwich tomorrow morning. You haven't brought me anything in over a week."

He was right, but I can't keep all these things in my mind at once. But I would tomorrow morning, because he was so appreciative, which was a rare trait in these parts. A little more banter, and I left for Tam Hiep.

Through the gate with no problem, down the path into the village, I walked over to Kim Lon's house, but she wasn't in, nor was Hoa who often was with one of the village kids who looked after her, so took a seat at the stand and ordered a beer, feeling pretty good.

Not a bad weekend so far, but don't get cocky, I told myself, everything ends. Halfway through my beer, Omar showed up.

"Omar, where you been?" "Normal operations," he said, "no excitement. Look for Lanh for excitement," he said laughing. "She number one girl."

Interesting, I thought. Omar had a tendency to judge girls by their sexual prowess, their gymnastic-styled movements, and of course their friendliness. He was a little like Banks with the heels behind the ear trick Me, I was slower and didn't feel that I knew Kim Lon well enough to pursue those kinds of "kinetic" movements. For me at this point, I just loved the "missionary." What a wonderful way to pray…a vast improvement over the teachings of the nuns. Lanh showed up and Omar rose to leave.

"Maybe next time we have beer and some talk," he said. "Sure." I answered, "I've got a good story for you." With that, they left. I checked back at Kim's house who wasn't in so hoofed it back home. Considering the possibilities, everything had worked out rather well for the weekend.

CHAPTER 13

THEY'D been bugging me at the Orderly Room to put in for an R&R. The thing is I don't really want one. From what the boys who have taken them have told me, it's the same as being here. Drinking and fucking. I can see why guys from the field are into it, but the way I had been living included enough of that on a daily basis to leave no desire to go elsewhere.

Some of them liked Hawaii, especially the married ones. They could hook up with their wives. Others made it that far with the military and then flew home via civilian carrier for a few days. I was getting so comfortable with my work and my Tam Hiep life with Kim Lon and my regular runs to Saigon to see Paul that I'd just as soon skip it. Why rock the boat? Maldonado and Flores were usually in the club about that time, so I thought I'd stop over and talk with Flores who had just returned from Bangkok.

I saw they're both sitting at the bar in the company club, so I pulled up a stool beside Flores. "How you guys doing?" I asked. "Mostly you, Flores, I see your partner twice most every day. How was Bangkok?"

"It was great, man; plush hotels, girls available at all the clubs, good food every meal, cheap beer." He went on and on, and all I could think of was that it's better than that right here where we're living. I don't like plush. I don't care for the high end.

"What do you think, Maldi?" Might as well get his take. "You going to go there on an R & R?"

"I don't know," he answered, "I like my day-to-day life here, even though I don't run around much and I'm no big drinker. I don't know. Maybe."

"I don't know either." I said. "Thanks boys, I've gotta be going."

Two weeks later, I was on the plane with Mooers on the way to Bangkok. He talked me into it. The funny thing was I'd put in for Australia much earlier, but it had never opened up for R&R tours. Just after I agreed to take in Bangkok with Mooers, notice came that I was approved for Australia. I panicked. I didn't know how to deal with White girls. Without drink, I was afraid of them. I might as well admit it to myself. So taking the easy way out, the comfortable way out, Mooers and I were flying around Cambodia for Bangkok. Must be that over flying Cambodia wasn't legal. But they didn't mind slipping in a few bombs now and then, not the US Airforce.

I was also thinking I had to get the girl from Tam Hiep out of my mind or this whole trip wasn't going to play. It'll be a digression back to the short time days, the three-dollar girls you hardly know. I was talking with Carl about it, but he was ambivalent.

"Don't sweat it, Collins. We're too young. We need life…and I'll help you," said Carl Mooers, "This is going to work out."

One good thing was we met a taxi driver named Norm who wanted us to sign him on for the week. He'd do us exclusively for a few bottles of whiskey and cartons of cigarettes that we could pick up cheap at a small PX that seemed to exist only for the R&R GIs.

By the time we got in late that night, with a couple of pretty Thai chicks, I was wondering what kind of operation this man's army was pointing us toward. If you're a farm kid who reads a bit, you know R&R means rest and recuperation from active duty, so this must be the official version. In Vietnam, they've got two set ups that I'm aware of for that purpose. China Beach in Da Nang, and Vung Tau on the old Cap St. Jacques beaches a couple of hours from Saigon. The GIs lucky enough to have an in-country R&R get to swim and lie around the beaches. Drink beer and play volley ball. Kind of like an all American summer weekend. I was sure there're some girls around but nothing like here in Bangkok. This place was mechanized.

This looks like production line sex. Across the street from the hotel is a four-story massage house. A rub down and everything that goes with it our driver Norm says.

"You name it, Steam and Cream, hot bath and soap suds with the girl or maybe two girls in the tub." He goes on and on. But didn't mention the string of golden balls as per Kama Sutra. I'm sure they must be more sophisticated here than Mai Le back in Bien Hoa with her knotted rag…or let's hope so.

"You know what, Mooers, do you think we'll be doing any tourist type things here or is it going to be like going to Bien Hoa or Saigon back home…

drinking and fucking? It'd be nice to look around the country a little. Pick up come culture, you know what I mean."

"You don't worry about that" chimed in Norm. "I can show you real culture…just stick with me."

"Ok, man, first thing in the morning…we'll hit it."

I have this girl with me named Malee who is quite beautiful, great on English, and very willing. Earlier, Norm had dropped us off at a club that was packed with beautiful girls who all had numbers pinned to their tops. I asked about number twelve to the bartender after many drinks and late into the evening. He said "fine, if she likes you." She did and she was with me now for the night. Twelve dollars for twenty-three hours. That's the deal. Mooers is going up to his room with a girl named Lawan who he met in the same joint.

"Good luck," I yelled after him, "and be careful."

He turned and smiled and kept going. I followed along to my room with Malee. At least we were sensible enough to each have our own pad, or mattress might be more to the point.

After a whole night of sexual frenzy, Malee and I got ourselves together and joined Carl and Lawan in the hotel coffee shop. The girls started jabbering in Thai. Mooers began boasting of his sexual prowess, and I was thinking of Kim Lon and feeling a little guilty. I mean, we didn't have any kind of arrangement or anything like that, but there it was. Guilt.

"Hey, Carl, I'm beginning to feel out of sorts about this screwing around. You know my feelings for the girl in Tam Hiep."

"You fucking nut. She's probably got more boyfriends than you had girlfriends in your whole life and probably also has a husband."

"Don't be mean, Carl, you ass hole, I think I might love her."

"Talk to Malee, you idiot, and get with it. Soon you'll love her. We've only got five days here. Don't fuck it up with that kind of bull shit."

I knew he was right. I'd get with it. I saw Norm over in the corner talking to some local dudes and initiated a conversation. He said he'd be ready to head out for a tour around town whenever the girls left.

"Hey, Malee," I asked, "do you have a picture of yourself that I could have?" She said sure, for two bucks. It was a good one, so I had no problem paying up. After all, these girls need their money. Who knows how many men get a cut of that original twelve bucks? She rattled off in Thai to the local men Norm was visiting with. They all started laughing. I asked Norm what they were laughing about.

"The two bucks you paid her for the picture," he said, "and the guy laughing the hardest is her husband."

"What the fuck!" That set me back, but apparently here in Bangkok, it's just a wife working out for some extra money. Back on the farm, "working out" meant just that, a job off the farm to pick up some extra cash to keep things going.

"Listen," it was Carl. "Let's drop all this shit and get moving. My R&R is getting shorter and shorter by the minute."

We took off with Norm and drove the streets of Bangkok for the rest of the day. It was somewhat interesting but to me nothing like Saigon. It was too clean and modern. No jeeps, no APCs, no Huey's; it was boring. But… so far, at least the girls and the Singha beer were great.

We were sitting with Norm down along a canal in a native market having one of those Singha beers. Carl was once again onto describing his last night gymnastics with Lawan.

Carl's great love is eating pussy. He won't shut up about it…the war is drifting.

"She loves me for that you know, that Lawan. I think I'll try and get her again for tonight. She's a proven girl. Why take a chance on another?"

"Well, I'm going to keep my eyes open for one ever more beautiful." What a jerk, I thought. I missed my home across the road from Tam Hiep in Vietnam and was still wondering why I was there.

"Hey, Norm, why are we sitting here in this market that's just like the riverside market in Bien Hoa? You must know of some modern-day lunch spot with live entertainment or something. Let's get moving."

Norm said he knew where to find anything we'd need. There was a great place nearby on the main drag where good food was available with great girl singers. And beautiful waitresses. We jumped in for the short ride over.

Norm's car was a '53 Pontiac in great condition. Probably just the type that attracts GI business. The restaurant was the bottom floor of a hotel.

"This better be something, Norm," I told him. "Looks pretty middle class to me."

"No problem, GI, because they have beautiful girl singer with beautiful voice. We ordered some beers and some food and waited for the girl. She was beautiful and had a great voice, but it was how she was dressed and what she sang that impressed me. Which made me wonder. Her name was Achara and she was dressed in colors. A multicolored blouse along with rainbow-striped hip-hugging bell bottom pants. She looked like girls who were appearing in articles published by *Time* magazine, the so-called hippie culture that was beginning to take hold in the States. She looked great, but her song was even more to the point. I'd never heard it before.

"If you're going to San Francisco, be sure to wear some flowers in your hair…" It really got me.

"Have you been to San Francisco?" I asked Carl. "Hell, no," he replied. "The only west coast stop I've ever made is at Travis on the way over here."

"We gotta get there." I said. "Maybe this will spread over the whole country…if we're lucky."

"I don't care what they call themselves as long as they look like this girl and dress like this girl. She's something else."

We were quiet after that…for some time. Both of us lost in thought. It's funny, the world changed when I came to Southeast Asia with the army. Upside down from anything I'd known, and it was looking like it might be the same when and if I ever got back there.

That night we were back at it, driving around Bangkok stopping in at various joints looking for the most beautiful…that we could buy for the next twenty-three hours. There's probably no justification for this kind of thinking, but it looked different to me here than it did in Vietnam. There we were all in the same boat. The girls and the GIs were all just ultimately trying to make it through to another day. Here, it was like a livestock auction. I knew cows and horses…but girls. That's something else. However, my conscience did not get the best of me.

"Listen, Norm," said Carl, "let's go back where we picked up the two girls last night. I want to see if Lawan is still around."

We returned to the Blue Lotus, bought some beers, and began looking around. It wasn't that late, but the girls who were left were all dancing with each other. It was a good display. Carl was able to locate Lawan, so happiness prevailed for him. I was talking to Chariya, a vivacious creature but not so beautiful. Just fun. She spoke great English.

"Where you from in the States?" she asked. There was never any question about who we were or where we had arrived in Bangkok from. Vietnam GIs stood out like a sore thumb.

"New York." I answered. "Not the City, way up north."

"I know, I know" she answered. "New York State. I met many GIs from there, and I have gone to school here. I know the world." Really, I was thinking. She's a nice girl.

Carl and I were chauffeured back to the hotel with the girls by our main man Norm and another night of pleasuring in Bangkok got underway. Mooers and Lawan went directly to their room. Chariya and I stopped in at the hotel coffee shop for a late night java. I noticed that her smaller fingers and toes were very much in the miniature. As they progressed down toward the smallest digit, they were hardly an inch long. I'd never seen that before.

"How come?" I asked her.

"All the time when I was a young girl and was growing up, people asked me that question. I can only say that I was born that way. So what?"

I assured her that I meant nothing by that, just curious. Chariya worked during the day as a secretary; however, the pay wasn't enough to keep her household going.

"I only go with man I like," she said, "like you. If I no like, get lost I tell him. Let's go to room."

We did as she suggested. I noticed there were a few couples around the pool as we walked to the elevator. I don't like pools in buildings…or outside. I like lakes.

I quickly undressed and stretched out on the bed and laid on my back to show off. She hardly noticed. She was humming and smiling. A very pleasant girl. I noticed an indentation on the edge of her stomach as she stood naked beside the bed.

"Chariya, what happened?" I asked. She turned around and showed me another on the opposite side of her body. "Bullet hole. When I am a child at my village in the countryside, somebody shoot me. I very sore for long time."

"Lucky he didn't kill you," I answered thinking that a bullet through the gut could be deadly as hell anywhere, especially in the backcountry over here.

"Come close to me," she said. And we began the age-old game of fucking…or rather working up to it. She's a sweet girl, nuzzling me and moaning over me. When I finally slip inside her, she grabs right ahold of me with her pussy and it clicked. My God, a snapping pussy, just like the old lifer sergeants always told me about, saying if you ever find one don't ever let her go. I couldn't at the moment if I'd wanted to. She had a good grip on me, one that would only weaken after an explosion, which shortly occurred…and then she herself screamed with pleasure. We both slept hard till morning.

"How was she?" Carl asked, "Good as the night before?"

We were down in the hotel coffee shop for morning java. Both girls had returned home, and it wasn't clear if they had kids or were taking care of others in the family. I had told Chariya that I hoped she would stay with me for the rest of the week. She said she'd be in touch.

"Better than you could ever imagine, Carl, my boy. My first real snapper."

He laughed and said the world's full of them.

"All the women who you get on with well are eventually that way. There's no secret. The old lifers are full of shit."

I wasn't sure of that, but he might have had a point. What did I know? You don't learn much about women pulling teats on Holsteins.

For the rest of the week, I stayed with Chairya, one of the sweetest girls I'd ever met. Carl picked up a different girl every night and was quite proud of himself. He hadn't been pursuing much along that line in Vietnam.

I must say that Chairya was a lovely girl. All the Thai girls were, but I longed for the countryside of Vietnam, the village of Tam Hiep and my real girl, Kim Lon, the dusky-skinned one who hailed from Cambodia.

CHAPTER 14

NOBODY was hurt, but our luck soon turned the other way. We were a man short supplying the detail for the Ammo Dump patrol, so Captain Dewey picked me. I explained that normally I was exempt from this kind of duty because of my KP responsibilities. He laughed and said that was his call and that I shouldn't forget he was the boss there.

"You tell Maldonado to make the runs tonight and tomorrow morning. You'll be back in time for the ration pick up." OK, I did that, picked up my M-14 and what other gear I needed and jumped on the truck. There was a surprising change since I'd been out in the field here. Most of the brush had been cleared, and fencing with guard towers had been erected. Nothing too fancy, but much more sensible than the previous set up. It must be that they were sick of getting it blown and someone with some brains took a look at it. The sun was approaching the horizon, which set the scene for a rather enjoyable ride to the far perimeter.

Right off, four of us were dropped off at one of the towers. The gig was, two stayed up in the tower and two stayed awake on the ground in a sandbagged fox hole. For us that meant one man stayed awake in each spot and the other got some sleep. In theory it all worked out.

The Sgt. of the Guard let us make the choices where we'd be spending the night. He preferred that we alternate but after dark who would know. He couldn't possibly remember all the positioning of troops. There were dozens of us. The bigger problem here was that there was no way to hide out like in the old days before the brush was gone and the fencing with towers didn't exist. Now they could drive along the perimeter road and harass the hell out of us. Banks and I pulled the tower. We volunteered for it and told the other two whom we had never met that we'd stay for the night. The fox hole was hotter than hell.

The night progressed nicely enough till two or three o'clock when you really get tired. I was on, and Banks was sitting on the floor of the tower leaning against the wall snoozing a little. We were perhaps thirty feet in the air, and it was a very quiet night. Not even any bombing going on. Ordinarily, the rolling thunder of B-52s could be heard off in the west. There were no birds, of course maybe all you'd see at this time of night was owls, and I don't even know if they had them here. At any rate, there was not much life left after a good spraying. I was tired, nodding off some when I looked down and saw a jeep stopped with no one in it. I gave Banks a kick, and he woke up, but he wasn't on his feet when the Captain of the Guard stuck his head up above the ladder.

I immediately wondered why he hadn't checked with the guys on the ground before climbing the ladder, but apparently, he hadn't, the bastard. At any rate, Banks was awake if not on his feet, so I figured it wouldn't matter. Something awakened the men on the ground, and they yelled up at us. The Captain was pissed off but didn't say a great deal. Just took all of our names. We knew he hadn't caught the men on the ground and technically hadn't caught either myself or Banks, though we did indeed look very sleepy. The Captain spoke a few nasty words and left.

"The fucker better not turn me in alls I can say," said Banks. "I've a two-week AWOL Article 15 pending. You put 'em both together and you got a court martial. I don't need no stockade time. It ain't good time as far as the year goes either, you get my drift, Collins?"

"Yup. But it's a couple of hours before we're done with this shift, so maybe let me get some shut eye. You can't sleep now at any rate, right?"

"How the fuck could I? They might lock me up."

I reminded him that a couple of weeks ago, Pacheco had been pulled off one of the towers after nodding out from the half dozen joints he'd smoked, one after the other. He hadn't mentioned any repercussions over that thus far. I drifted off after that and came to hearing Adrian Cronauer yelling "Gooooooood morning, Vietnam," which was a great way to wake up, especially after such a fucked-up night.

After riding back in and grabbing a quick shower, I hooked up with Maldonado to pick up the rations hoping that last night had been my finale back on that particular detail.

"No trouble at all, Collins, when you were gone, none at all. Flores rode with me at night. He loved it. He's sick of driving for the Captain. Too boring playing straight. He loved being around the girls."

"That's great, and thanks a lot. My run up north worked out fine too." I decided I'd wait a few days before leading into him covering me, clandestinely, for three days again, if Kim Lon had a way for me to travel with her to Cambodia. When we were finished with the rations, I made Pacheco a super egg sandwich, even found some blue cheese for topping, and found him hanging out in the shade by the motor pool.

"Collins, you're my man, I love you…as long as you keep these sandwiches coming. They don't cook anything like this in the mess hall, "said Pacheco. "Keep 'em coming and thanks, many thanks."

I told him it was only because he was so appreciative and then asked him if he'd heard anything about him being pulled off the guard tower for sleeping.

"Not yet, and I think that Mooers did some finagling in the Orderly Room to tone that down. Haven't heard nothing and this far out shouldn't. Gotta keep my nose clean for the duration here."

"That'd be a good idea" I told him, and then relayed the experience Banks and I had last night. Pacheco wished us good luck but seemed more involved with his sandwich. I went back to the hooch and got some sleep.

Some days later in Tam Hiep, I managed to find Kim Lon and Hoa at home.

"Ah, my friend you," she said laughing. "No I remember your name, Collins, Private Bill Collins, for sure I do. I just kidding." Often, these girls here used "you" in place of a GI's name; which they frequently forgot. I didn't want her to forget mine.

"Kim, don't you joke. It makes me afraid you forget me." "Never happen, Collins, you know that." "I hope so, you sweet thing. I could never forget you. How about a soda at the stand? Maybe some snails for Hoa."

We walked over and found Omar and Lanh there joking around. The girls started jabbering; Hoa had her snails, and Omar and myself started talking GI.

"I had a good run to Da Nang, Omar, easier than I thought. All the rides worked out, and I found both of my cousins. Fun."

"My family have bad luck ," he began. "You know I tell you I have uncle who is Col. In the N VA. He die. Americans bomb his unit up north between

Au Shau Valley and Cambodia. Maybe Lao, I don't know up there so good. He big shot and should not be near bombing but somehow it happen. We don't know so much down here in South. Have cousin with VC up near DMZ and he hear on NVA radio transmissions from Hanoi."

"How did they get word to you and your family down here?" I asked. "There is no way to send letters is there."

"My cousin have friends in ARVN who pass the word down. There is always a way in Vietnam, Collins, you know for sure."

He had a point. The Vietnamese grapevine, as it was tagged by someone in the US State Department back in the 1950s, got to be known as the "fastest form of communication known to mankind" and that point seemed to be made on a regular basis.

"I'm sorry for you, Omar. Such bad luck for your family."

"Yes, Lanh too. She come from the village of Ben Suc and you know the Americans destroy that village during Junction City so her family no have home now. They live in refugee camp. It no good. She can help a little bit but not enough."

There is no end to the sad stories you can hear in Tam Hiep, or from the girls working in the Mess Hall. Sometimes, I think they don't care who wins; they just do not want any more war.

Hoa was playing with some of the other village young girls, so Lanh said she'd hang out there longer and watch her. Kim and I headed down the trail for her little house.

"How long can you leave Hoa?" I asked Kim. "Long enough," she smiled.

It didn't take long to find ourselves stretched out tightly together on her bed. She had such firm, sensitive breasts, like the rest of her body which oozed solid muscle, hot muscle from within. We didn't talk for some time afterwards. I was in a trance. We hadn't been together for some days, and I realized I was getting in deeper after every time with her.

"Soon I have to go to Cambodia to see my father as I talk you before," she said quietly. "Can we go as we talk one time before?"

"Maybe." I said, "if I can find a way where it is possible with no trouble. I know that you will have to find how I can cross the border both ways that

135

I can believe before I can tell you. I think the chance of trouble is only at the borders. We can come up with excuses before and after the crossings."

Kim, I believed, did not appreciate the danger I'd be putting myself into traveling with her across an international border without the proper papers. Privates in the army were not issued passports. I hardly knew what one was. It wasn't needed crossing back and forth to Canada, and that's the only border I'd ever crossed. Travelers I'd known referred to Montreal as a European City and I'm sure it was, but I had no way of knowing. Europe was eons away from my pre army experience. After snuggling as long as she could before looking up Hoa, I told her I'd work on my end and she should work on hers. I'd like to go but didn't want to end up in the Stockade or worse.

"Omar, let me ask you something?" He had stayed after Kim and Lanh left with Hoa, so we had one last beer for the night. "Kim wants me to travel to Cambodia with her for two days. What do you think?"

"I think bull shit, man. If they catch you nothing but trouble. Stockade. If they catch you in Cambodia, nothing but very big trouble. No way can you do," said Omar.

I thought for a minute. "You know Omar it's kind of funny. You can cross the border to shoot people if you're under orders with the Army, but you can't cross for a cup of coffee with a girlfriend."

"Go tell Chaplin, GI, that be the real world."

That's how we left it after parting and walking in our separate directions. I knew Omar was right; however, the possibility of adventure was strong. And fuck it man, I'd been so lucky so far. You hate to quit and get beaten by the Green Machine.

Back riding along with Maldonado on the early morning a week later, we ran into real trouble. Along the old highway from Bien Hoa to Ho Nai, just beyond the US/ARVN POW stockade and as we were following another KP truck, this one from the 66th Supply Co blew up. Following the explosion, the deuce-and-a-half ran off the edge of the road intact but burning fiercely. We could see the girls leaping from the rear tailgate. The front of the truck wasn't visible. The roadway surface was intact, so the cause could not have been a mine. No suspicious characters were in sight. Maldonado applied brakes quickly, and our girls had immediately jumped ship to lend a helping hand to the girls from the other truck. My old front seat companion Hue was in the rear and was helping one victim to her feet. I ran over to see if she had picked up any info.

"This girl say there nothing bad, everything quiet, then boom. She don't know." I looked up and saw Maldonado had run up and checked the driver who was lying on the grass nearby. I went around to the other side of the truck to see if anyone was riding shotgun. A body was visible leaning on the dash enveloped in flames and not moving. It didn't look good, and the heat was too intense to get any closer. Finally, another jeep pulled up. The LT on board was already on the radio. He finished and ran over to me.

"I can't get closer. Too hot." I told him. He reached into the jeep for a fire extinguisher which he then sprayed on the side of the truck enough for us to pull the body out. The soldier was gone. He had no need for the dust off that was settling in just down the road. He must have been flying nearly overhead when they'd received the call for help.

Hue ran over yelling that there were two injured from the truck that needed help. By then, a medic from the dust off was close by, and he ran over to Hue. I went back to the chopper for a stretcher. Together, we loaded up the three wounded, and in minuets, they were off to the 93rd Evac. The LT found time to ask some questions at this point.

"Were you a witness to this happening?" he asked.

I gave him my version of what happened, which wasn't much help. I told him that I hadn't seen anyone nearby that looked suspicious and pointed out that the roadbed hadn't been damaged by the explosion, so it couldn't have been a mine. I did have a possibility though.

"If you look at the truck, LT, you'll see that most of the damage seems to be around the floor and door of the passenger side just above the gas tank.

"Looks like that's what exploded." I said. "But why?" he asked. I had an idea from stories I'd heard about leaving a vehicle parked alone anywhere outside of an army compound.

"You ever heard of the grenade trick? I asked him. He said no. "They take a grenade and tape the spoon with a couple of turns of electrical tape and then pull the pin and drop it into the gas tank. In short order, the tape will dissolve enough to release the spoon and the thing blows up. That could of happened."

"Makes sense," he said. "I'll get army investigators on it and take if from here." I told him I had to get going but left my name and company. Maldonado and I loaded our girls back in the truck and got talking as we drove on.

"It doesn't make any sense to me." I told him. "We've never seen that kind of trouble before, not at all. We don't even have our guns with us. Fuck it, the CO will be on our ass for that when we get back you can believe."

"I'm just glad we didn't get out asses blown to shit," was all that he said. "I don't give a good flying fuck about the CO's opinion. He can shove it. We handled everything just right there. We deserve a medal."

"Don't expect one," I said. "They'll probably threaten us with an Article 15 for leaving the post unarmed."

"The most they can say to us is that we're an hour late and that ain't much considering what just happened. That poor fuck in the truck. He was just having a pleasant morning drive and look how it ended. We've been lucky bastards."

"Let's hope it keeps up." I said.

That evening all the boys were in the club drinking and asking for the scoop on what happened.

"I told you them gooks were gonna hit a KP truck sooner or later," said Crow. "Just like back home in West Virginia. You can't trust the guy over in the next holler, how the fuck you gonna trust these gooks. You know they're all VC."

"Hey, come on, Crow, they know better. If nothing else, these girls bring home money and food. Why fuck it up? It doesn't make sense. I think some ass hole got it into his head to blow up an army truck and the bad luck hit them. Who knows, maybe the investigators will turn up something."

"Don't believe it," said Banks. "I've been in the army long enough to know that they can't find out nothing."

"They might find out enough to put you in the Stockade," I said not meaning to be mean.

Carl chimes in with "There's papers in the orderly room suggesting a summary court martial for you, Banks. I don't know the status but be warned. I don't even think they needed investigators."

That shook Banks up some, so we changed the subject to short time girls, "snapping pussy," and ordered another round of beers. Luckily, we left Miss Mai and Mai Ly alone with their professions. I was worried about Banks. He had a two-week AWOL last month that hadn't been dealt with, and if they pinned the sleeping on guard gig on him, he might end up in the Stockade. Neither of us had heard anything of that incident as the captain had left the guard tower that same night.

Carl asked if I'd read *The Green Berets*, which was recently published and was popular with the GIs, those who could read. That got a laugh but not from Crow, who did have trouble reading.

"Don't laugh at me, you college boy fuckhead," he shot back at Carl, a mild mannered guy who had gone for the laugh not meaning to be mean.

"Whadda you mean?" said Carl, "I flunked out after the first year. I ain't no college boy."

"Well, you know," said Crow, "that after beginning my fourth year in eighth grade I quit, but that don't mean I can't read, just means I don't like school."

"Let's drop it boys," I said, trying to defuse what could become a volatile situation. "There's not a great deal of brilliance in this whole crowd, so let's get back to basics, and the better qualities of short time girls. In fact, I've got to hang it up. A long day and I'm tired as hell. See you guys later."

The picture of the poor guy who had been killed in the truck stuck in my mind. Me and the people I hang around with have been lucky as hell. The only "bagged and tagged" thus far were Sparks and Easy.

Kim Lon wouldn't let up on Cambodia. After a session with her on the mattress, it was difficult to disagree on anything, but I in no way wanted to join Banks in the Stockade. That's what happened with him. After a Summary Court Marshall where myself and the captain who wrote us up both testified, he was given thirty days. The captain lied, or at least stretched the truth. He did not catch Banks sleeping. It might be technical, but sleeping and looking as if you'd been sleeping are not the same thing, as I testified, but who would take a private's word against an officer's? I knew Banks could take thirty days without batting an eye, but it was bad time and he'd owe the army.

Kim wasn't worried about anything like that. Her issues were life and death and enough food to stay alive. Most everything else was irrelevant.

"They feed you in the stockade, don't they?" she said, "so no problem. Just when you no have. When we go Cambodia, Collin?"

She had a point about food, but I still was worried about taking the chance or crossing the border…I'd never pushed things that far. What if I got stuck in Cambodia, and they wouldn't let me back into Vietnam? What the hell would I do then? I'd be a fucking deserter. They might shoot me. My immediate solution was to hitch down to see Paul the next morning after picking up rations. Get his opinion. If I was late returning, Maldonado would handle things.

It was another beautiful morning in Vietnam as he dropped me off at the main gate, and I looked up and down the highway. North led to 11 Field Forces and south directly to Saigon. This morning "direct to Saigon" seemed less complicated as I began hoofing it south. As always, a jeep pulled over.

"Where you heading?" I asked the driver, a PFC. "I'm going to the Newport Docks to pick up some parts that were red lined for the motor pool."

"That'll work for me." I answered. "Going to see a friend near the airport."

An uneventful ride to the bridge where I disembarked and immediately caught another ride in an army sedan, with a driver for a chaplain who was heading there to pick up his boss. First time I was ever in a civilian/military vehicle.

Paul was still in bed, believe it or not. I kicked it, and he opened his eyes, blinked his eyes was more to the point.

"For Christ's sake, Bill, can't you let an important Spec. 5 like me get some sleep?"

"How the hell did you get promoted? You don't do shit here, just cover your ass."

"That's all you have to do, you ass hole. You haven't figured that out yet? I'm back on a detail now, a night shift over at Tan Son Nhut, where I can get some sleep most nights. A great gig. If you want to go downtown, OK, but let's hit the dining room first for coffee."

On the cyclo riding down to Tu Do St., we discussed my Cambodia idea.

"You're fucked up if you do that," said Paul. "Big trouble if you're caught. It's supposed to be classified, but a couple of weeks ago, I made a trip to Phnom Penh in a C-123. I mean this was undercover. They made me wear civilian clothes with nothing that would identify me as being with the American Military. You know Cambodia is supposed to be neutral, and we're not involved there at all militarily."

That brought to mind Wilton from the 25th Infantry who told the story at the Ammo Dump one night about a mission into Cambodia where they wiped out a village. No military like hell.

"At any rate, I made it there and back without any ID but was under the protection of the military all the time. You won't be. And I didn't have to cross any border or go through customs. You won't be that lucky. Don't do it, man, it's not worth that kind of risk just to make a girl happy. You looking to marry her or something?"

"Hell no," I said. I was in no way going to bare my feelings about Kim Lon to anyone else. "It's just an idea at this point. Keeping things interesting."

"Speaking of Cambodia, you been up to Cu Chi lately? It's on the way, isn't it?"

"It's halfway to the river, and yes, I was up with the 25th last week. Their new photo interpreter needed some practical help. Got up in the air once in a Birddog and actually flew right up to the border where we made a couple of low passes and did take some ground fire. A couple of holes in the wing was about it. I'm lucky like you."

"Sounds like fun. If Sandy is at the bar, maybe I'll check it out with him."

We chugged along the same old route, past the VN white house, left toward the Cathedral with the US Embassy in view down the street on the left and then right down Tu Do till we were dropped off at the Continental. I liked to start walking here, so I could check out the people on their deck, "the Continental Shelf." No big shots visible today, but as luck would have it, no lack of beautiful women, most of them locals. I kept thinking I'd run into Holly again, the girl who worked at the Australian Embassy.

"Hey, Paulie, you ever run into that girl Holly again, the red head from the Australian Embassy? She looked doable."

"I would hope so," he said, "otherwise, what a waste. I don't care what color they are as long as they are young, beautiful, and willing. A good soldier's dream."

"You're afraid of White women now, you know it. Not me, man, that's you. You're afraid of 'em. You were back home."

"I'm learning though." I said smiling. It was true. I was a sorry excuse for a womanizer back in the world. But I was learning.

Amazingly, the traffic on Tu Do was light, even the foot traffic, and I always wondered why. This was the best strip in the country. We walked down past the Air France office and turned right on Nguyen Hiep for the Kangaroo. Like most times when I stopped in, Sandy was there.

"How's it going, boys?" he said. "You Yanks doing much fighting, or are you leaving it all to us?"

"We're just observing the war, Sandy. Very exhilarating." I didn't want to compete with him on "the great war." The Aussies do a year in Vietnam and then a year in Malaya to carry on the "good fight" there. They got us outnumbered. We ordered a round of beer from Tot and inquired about Kanh.

"Kanh have boyfriend Australia," said Tot, "she busy now at home. Only work here some time."

"Good for her but who can Paulie talk with? Him need girlfriend. Buy tea." That would really piss Paul off. He was one of those cheap bastards who would have to be pushed hard to buy a girl a tea. Against his principals.

"I'll find my own girlfriend, Bill. Worry about yourself." This was getting like back on the farm. Mocking each other.

"Hey, Sandy, how's Malaya. You were there before here, weren't you?"

"It's great, more settled than this place, after all the Brits have been there a long time, and they don't like to be thrown out. I don't know why the fuck we're fighting for them, but there we were. However, in Malaya, we have Singapore. We have Bugis Street. Hard to beat for a whore strip, mate. Plenty of transvestites. Anything you want."

I was wondering then what could be the Singapore version of "Mai Ly of the knotted wash rag" and was going to ask him but then thought better of it. Knowing the Asian multitude of sexual skills, he'd probably top me.

"My last tour there, I picked up an old Jaguar convertible, XK-120, and lived within cruising distance of Singapore. A great fucking time, mate. When I leave here, I'm going back and then leave from there for home."

"I've got a question for you, Sandy, ever been to Cambodia?"

"Why go there, but no I haven't. Never had a chance. Too bad Flynn isn't here because he goes frequently. All the civilian residents who have freedom of movement use Phnom Penh for a R&R town. Supposed to be great. Why, you going?"

I told him about my friend Kim Lon and her interest in my traveling with her on her next trip. I figured Maldonado could cover me for three days like he did on my run to Da Nang. He'd have to do it without help this time, but I was sure he could handle it. The problem I hadn't figured out was back and forth across the border.

"Once again, too bad Flynn isn't here. He might have old photographer papers you could adapt to fit you that would work. Much of the time these wogs ain't too keen on paperwork. Just slip 'em a few bucks."

"You think he'll be around soon? Maybe you could ask him next time he's here. I could try and return the favor."

"Yea, I will. Don't worry about the favor. He doesn't give a shit about that, I'm sure he'd be glad to help you out. Me, I wouldn't go. Too risky."

"I might not, but I hate to pass up a little adventure. Be something different."

We shot the breeze for another hour putting down some beers in the process before cruising back up to Paul's place. Before leaving, I said I'd likely be back soon to see if Sandy had picked up papers that would be useful.

Rides were few and far between on the route home. I walked most of the way to the Newport Bridge before picking up a short ride as far as the ARVN war memorial and then walked again till after dark. Finally, a deuce-and-a-half pulled over, and I jumped on. It didn't stay peaceful. Not a mile past, the memorial gunfire was heard over the rice paddies on the right. Momentarily, gunships flew in blasting rockets. I couldn't make out if the target was people or houses, but in short order, a Puff, the Magic Dragon, showed up on the scene with its ray guns piercing straight to the ground. I'm thinking if it's VC in the field, they're fucked. Supposedly, this thing can cover a football field-sized area with bullets most every square inch. No action within 500 feet of the road, so after slowing for the show, we drove on.

I jumped off at the 66th Supply gate and walked to the club. The usual suspects were there, except for Banks who was doing his thirty days.

"I'm going to turn you in," said Carl, "You've been AWOL again, I'm sure of that."

"Just visiting within the Army," I said. "If that isn't legal, it should be. Don't start acting like a 'candy striper'; you'll get popped in the face."

I was kidding of course. He'd been one in Basic he'd told me, and some trainee had punched him out. Said it was the last time he'd volunteered for anything. I felt like looking up Kim but didn't want to get into the Cambodia deal without having made a decision and figured out if I was going.

"You know what," Santimaw said, "I just extended for six months. Going home for thirty days in two weeks."

"Why?" I asked. "What's up?"

"I might as well. Got another year to do after leaving and I like it here. Who wants to go back to Ft. Benning or Gordon, of heaven forbid Ft. Polk? That's supposed to be the shit hole of the army. They'd probably send me there. If this all works out, I'm going to extend on return till I've less than ninety days left and then get out. Anyhow I've got to check in on my wife. I heard she's screwing around."

"Like you haven't" I said laughing. "Fuck you," he said, "I'm a man. She's a acting like a whore if that's going on." Enough of that for me. I headed for the hooch and went to sleep.

CHAPTER 15

IN the end, Kim made up my mind for me. She said, "Let's go, it be fun." So that was that. I'd prepared Maldonado for the possibility but not the date. He felt he could handle it, keep the work done, and make excuses for my absence without getting into it too much. Mooers in the Orderly Room said he'd keep his eye open and cover me at that end as much as possible. I'd made one other precaution just in case. My sister had sent me two green fifties, one for each way on the border if it came to it.

This trip was nothing out of the ordinary for Kim Lon. She made it most every month, and the usual mamasan looked after Hoa. I spent the early part of the night before leaving with Kim but no love making. I was too nervous.

"What the matter, Bill Collins, my friend. You no love Kim anymore?" she said laughing. She had no interest either, I could tell.

"You don't fool me," I said, "you're nervous too." The fact of the matter was that if I was picked up and she was with me, we'd both be in for it.

"OK, Kim, I'm leaving now. Tomorrow I will be ready to leave at 6:00. I'll be here with civilian clothes, and we can catch the bus from Tam Hiep to Saigon at 6:20, and we are off, for good or ill."

"What be ill?" she asked. I didn't bother answering.

Once again, the guard at the main gate started giving me a hard time, so I told him to fuck off and walked down to the RMK-BRJ entry point for civilian workers. The Vietnamese guy on there just smiled and waved me through. Great people.

The bus was overflowing in Tam Hiep as we pulled out for Saigon. I mean crowded. My legs would be numb before reaching the downtown bus station, which took over an hour. The Phnom Penh bus was a little better but not much. It figured to be safe enough till reaching the border. That would be the main test.

While stopping in at the Kangaroo when driving through town on a quick detail last week, I had been able to obtain one of Flynn's outdated ID cards from Sandy. My boy Carl had switched pictures with office paraphernalia from the Orderly Room. This wouldn't ordinarily pass muster without the accompanying passport but that was what the green fifty was for.

My nervousness was wearing off, as Kim and I sat in the front seat of the bus leaving Saigon. We were holding hands and feeling like a million dollars. A grand adventure with enough danger to make it interesting.

After a rather slow drive through the morning traffic, we reached the outskirts of Saigon. This was a new road for me. Next town Cu Chi.

Cu Chi was packed with military vehicles from the 25th Infantry, which was beginning to make me nervous. The civilian clothes made me feel like a spy or a traitor or something. All I wanted was to clear this last American outpost without being stopped and asked for ID. The traffic lessened considerably leaving town heading west.

"Why you scared?" laughed Kim. "We have no trouble, I tell you."

"Ok for you to say." I said, "but if they pull me off this bus, and I get turned over to any kind of authority, I'm toast. You however can just ride along and see your father."

"What be toast?" asked Kim. "It's nothing, just an expression." The next thing would be what is expression. I wonder if I will be able to speak clearly with girls from the home country when and if I ever get out of here.

The next stop for the bus would be the ferry across the river, a branch of the Mekong, where there could possibly be a military checkpoint. And there was, but luckily being manned by ARVN troops who slowed the bus down to a crawl but then waved us through. From the ferry, it was less than ten miles to the border, the first potential for real trouble.

"Ok, Kim, you tell me what to do. You know how things go here."

"Sometimes, we all have to leave bus for checking out. Sometimes not. If we stay on, you play like sick, and I will make up something. If they want more, I show them fake press pass. If they want more, I slip them green money."

"And if that doesn't work, what the fuck then. I'll end up in a Cambodian jail."

"You no talk number ten with me, GI, you know who I am."

"Sorry, Kim Lon, I very sorry, just scared." which I was beginning to be and really to start wondering what the hell I was doing here. I could have been back pulling rations with Maldonado enjoying the morning run. We were next in line at the border. When stopped after a long talk with the driver, the patrol agent boarded the bus and somehow made his way through the crowd. The thing was packed with people and all kinds of things they were bringing into the country to resell or give to their relatives. He stopped at our seat and talked with Kim. I was hunched over against the window feigning sleep, moaning a little.

"He sick," said Kim to the agent. "I bring him to my father in Phnom Penh to see doctor."

"Papers for him," said the agent. Kim started fumbling through things and turned up the press pass.

"Where passport?" said the agent. Kim answered something to him in Khmer, and he jabbered something back and then moved on. Maybe. I kept pretending to be asleep till the bus began moving and then I breathed a sigh of relief. Thinking about it once on the road again, why would they care about a White man going to Phnom Penh? It was the R&R town for the foreign civilians who lived in Saigon, especially the foreign press. They spent money, real money in Phnom Penh, so why the hell not. That was the thinking I told myself.

As we neared town, I asked Kim where her father lived.

"He live on the Tonle Sap river but not so far up. Just outside of the city. Now he have small roadside stand like in Tam Hiep, along the way to Siam Reap. Before my mother die, we live on houseboat on the Tonle Sap lake. Very big lake with many fish. Many Vietnamese have lived this way for years. My father from Vietnam, but my mother Khmer. He so sad when she die that he leave and come here but don't do so well. That why I bring him money. You can see."

"I see, Kim, you never told me before about your family."

"You no ask," she said. "But now we go find father."

From the bus station, we boarded a trailer-like contraption being towed behind a motor bike and headed through town, a very attractive town. Wide streets and not nearly as crowded as Saigon. Many new buildings that must have been the doing of the present ruler Prince Sihanouk who fancied himself a Francophile, a saxophone player and a film maker, all of which he was.

The river front sported many interesting looking bars and restaurants. I was hoping that Kim's father didn't live that far away from this area. We were a long way off from Miss Mai's or Mai Ly's.

"Very soon we be there," said Kim. "My father's name is Oanh. I will call you to him, Collin. It better for him to say than Bill because I no like."

"You'd better like. What if we get married. You will not call me by my name?"

"Never happen GI. I too young."

"You're not too young to make love, Kim. Why too young to get married, for the moment? No more than that."

I wasn't proposing, just kidding with her. I never know what's really going on in her head."

"Here my father's place," she said, and we pulled off the road to a real shaky spot, not much more than a poor man's tool shed back on the farm. We weren't carrying much in the way of gifts. Apparently, her old man preferred cash, and I imagined Kim did much better than him, working for the GIs on Long Binh.

A grizzled old fellow came out to the serving counter and broke into a broad smile as he recognized his daughter. They hugged each other breaking into a Khmer jumble of words that of course to me meant nothing. Kim placed a beer and glass of ice on the counter for me and continued with her father. Eventually, another girl sat down. Another sixteen-year-old beauty who I tried to engage in conversation, but apparently, she spoke not a word of English.

"Her name is Boupha," said Kim noticing me with the girl. "She speaks a little bit English but is afraid to try so keep at it."

"Boupha, how are you?" I asked. She just smiled so I kept drinking beer. It was hotter than hell here. I wondered where we were going to sleep and also, I was thinking that if possible, I'd like to head back to the border tomorrow morning if she could be persuaded. I didn't have a good feeling about being "really" AWOL. Maybe they'd call it desertion since I'd left the country.

That could be a real problem. Kim eventually came around and sat down beside me with a coke for her and another beer for me.

"Where do we sleep?" I asked her. "There doesn't seem to be much room here."

"There isn't" she said, "but we can do. My father wants for us to stay with him. I know maybe you like hotel but no can do. He my father."

"Ok, that's fine with me. I know how it is, and it's only for the night. But let me ask you Kim, can we go back tomorrow morning?" She frowned at that and said nothing for a minute. Then "Why we go then so soon. My father will be sad." I explained my thoughts and worries which she listened to and seemed to be considering.

"Maybe we can take my father to a foreigner restaurant back down this road for dinner. It will cost more than we should spend, but he never do this before."

"I'd love to take you both to a fancy restaurant for dinner, Kim. Do not worry, I have enough money. Maybe we can go to Le Royal Hotel restaurant. It's where famous people like Somerset Maughan and Charlie Chaplin have stayed when visiting Cambodia."

"Who they?" asked Kim. I told her to never mind, that we'd find out when we went there later this evening. Actually, the sooner the better. She went in the back to talk it over with her father. For me, just coming here and getting back to Vietnam was my whole idea. A great story for the boys not to mention getting in better with Kim Lon.

Eventually, we hit the road for the Le Royal Hotel, top shelf in Phnom Penh, maybe even in all of Cambodia. The old man had a motorbike that we all three piled on to ride back down the river where he had told Kim he knew its location. As we approached downtown, there was a noticeable congregation of police and military in the vicinity of the hotel. Closer yet, I noticed White men in suits who looked American scanning the crowd that was building up including the buildings surrounding the area. With my lack of ID, there was no need in taking a chance on being involved with them. We bumped into a foreign newsman named Jon Swain who told us that Jackie Kennedy was staying at the hotel.

Fuck me dead, mate, as Sandy would say. How could this be happening? Swain told us that we ought to go down by the river and find a small touristy place, for complications could build up here. He was trying to get close enough to shoot some pictures for *Paris Match*. I mentioned meeting Sean Flynn in Saigon, but not that I was supposed to be him if someone needed my ID. Might as well keep that quiet. At any rate we left, avoided the White men who were probably Secret Service and ended up at the Foreign Correspondents Club, the FCC, on the riverside. It was full of a mix of locals and foreigners, which made it appealing to Kim and her old man. Almost like going out in Montreal or for me, NYC. I was a hick too.

"I love this," said Kim. "It very nice. Some very beautiful people. You see the clothes on those White women, so very beautiful." They were indeed however for me I just see the woman, The hell with the clothes. Kim was still dressed like a Tam Hiep girl and her father was worse off, and I wasn't much better, but we all had a great time. It was so pleasant in Cambodia, the "Gentle Land" of French and Asian literature. Maybe more pleasant when we got back to the old man's house and found a place to lie down, pressed tightly against each other. And that's the way it worked out. Rolling around covered with sweat on an old mattress tucked in behind the front counter in the throes of wild sex, and some passion too. We were so soaked afterward that we both ran out back naked down to the Tonle Sap for a rinse off in the river. After splashing around in the warm water, we got back at it in the grass along the shore. A more wonderful evening I couldn't remember. And with some luck, we'd be off tomorrow on the road to Saigon.

Kim left her father happy. He had the cash and dined out with the "big shots" in the foreigner restaurant along the quay. Ordinarily I suppose he lived pretty tight to the earth, period, no wasting money like last night.

The ride to the border was uneventful. No road blocks, just a very crowded bus, and we were told by the driver that they would be sure to empty the bus out at the Vietnam border crossing, which we were approaching.

"What do we do Kim?" I asked as the bus was pulled over.

She laughed and said "we do what he say. No can do otherwise."

The bus emptied out, and we were all lined up for passport checks. I was starting to worry like hell. This could be it. Kim had said to keep the fake press ID in my pocket with the green money under it so when the agent asked for the card, he had the cash in his hand. We'd hope for the best.

He came to me saying "Give me passport." I spread out my hands sort of expressing that I didn't have one and then handed him my packet. He looked at it and looked at me, then slid the pass card a bit to the side to expose a sliver of green, gave me a nasty look but kept on walking. I was clasping my ass to keep from gushing from the fear that this wouldn't work, that I'd be turned over to the MPs for court martial on charges of desertion. And wondering again why I had done this. The worry was for nothing. We were loaded back on the bus and off to the river. That had about finished me off.

As we drove along, Kim started laughing. I asked her what was so funny.

"You," she said. "You scared. If you live in Vietnam, you have real trouble to be scared of. Not this. You have bombs and guns and bullets and rockets. Napalm. Everything like that, so we don't get scared about border police."

"I understand but jail does scare me, and it would you too so there." It was all just small talk. I was so happy to be back in Vietnam, as if that could be possible, and it certainly was this time. The ferry across the river took longer than the ride in, so it was late afternoon when we arrived in Saigon. I'd thought we could perhaps go down on Tu Do Street and I'd show Kim around, but it was too late. She wanted to get back to Tam Hiep, so we waited around the terminal that was just pavement along the traffic circle across from the Ben Thanh Market till that bus was ready to leave, packed ourselves in for the trip home to Tam Hiep for her and Long Binh for me. I'd be glad to be back still hoping that I hadn't been missed by the 1st Sgt. or the CO. I walked Kim back to her house and hoofed it down the trail to the main gate. Pacheco was on guard.

"Where the fuck you been, asshole. The Captain is out to get you."

"What happened god damn it? I knew things were going too well."

"Maldonado didn't wake up on time this morning, and somehow your absence was noticed. Anyhow I'm warning you. Be careful. Make up some kind of plausible reason why you were gone. If they ever find out you've been to Phnom Penh, your ass is grass man. The stockade for you."

"Ok, Pacheco, is today's absence all that I have to explain myself for?"

"I think so," he said, "but remember you weren't there for that early morning run, so they know you've been gone since last night."

"Ok, I'll come up with something. Thanks a lot, and I had a great run to Cambodia."

I came up with a plan while walking back to the hooch. However, first I had to see Maldonado and then Carl in the Orderly Room to find out what the temperature was.

It was hot. He said the Captain was steaming and wanted blood, my blood.

"So, Collins," said Mooers, "what have you got for an explanation? If you can give me something, I can run it by him before he gets to you. This late it won't be till morning, so be sure you make the KP run with Maldonado along with the ration pickups. Make sense?"

"Sure, and I think I've a plausible story. I hitched a ride down to Saigon on a deuce-and-a-half from the front gate to 69 Dong Da St. to see my old friend from home Paul Savage. He's with the 4th Military Intelligence Battalion. They had a problem in Cu Chi where they man a detachment, so I rode along with him to check things out up that way. I'd never been there before. He had some kind of problem that held him till after dark, and we couldn't drive back. That road isn't open at night. He couldn't leave till midday, and by the time I hitched back up here, it was late. Obviously, I was AWOL; however, I was with the US military; consequently, it might be able for the Captain to overlook the whole thing. Maldonado covered me as far as the work went, and no one's the worse for wear. What do you think?" Carl looked at me rather oddly.

"How the hell did you come up with that? I know you went to Cambodia with that girl from Tam Hiep. What if he checks it out?"

"The odds are it would be too difficult. Paul could back me up at any rate. No problem there. If it doesn't work, well, screw it. I'll try another lie. No way I can admit to leaving the country. There's no evidence that I did. I don't care for lying, but man, survival is survival."

Carl started laughing. "If you get out of this, you fucker, you owe me fifty beers. It's not right. Most of us in our crowd, except for Banks, perform our given duties and hang around here drinking. We don't run all over hell looking for trouble."

"Who the hell's looking for trouble? I'm just living. This is the first time I've been out in the world, and I'm not going to spend the whole time working and drinking beer. There's a hell of a lot more out there."

"OK," said Carl. "I've got your back. If you don't hear from me, come to the orderly room tomorrow after you've picked up rations. The Captain should be there."

I thanked him profusely and headed down to the club for a beer. It'd been a long day. Banks and Santimaw as usual were there drinking away. They both looked up as I entered then started laughing.

"You're fucked," said Banks. You're gonna end up in the Stockade like me."

"Nope. Mooers has me covered. We got it all figured out. I'll see if it works tomorrow when I meet with Captain Dewey."

"Whatever," said Santimaw. "Tell us about Cambodia."

I ordered a round of beers and told them the whole story, which looking back on wasn't all that much. Just going there and returning without getting caught was the deal. Hardly any drinking, and in no way was I going to delve into my sexual relationship with Kim Lon. None of their business, but more than that, they'd make a joke out of it. It wasn't a joke to me.

"How about you guys, anything going on out in the Ammo Dump?"

"A sapper was shot crawling through the concertina on the far fence line, but nothing came of it. Just one more dead gook is how they wrote it up. The odd thing was he had no clothes on. We figure they go in naked first to figure out a safe route without risking getting their clothes hooked on a barb and then return dressed with a charge for one of the pads."

They had nothing else of interest to me, so I left them drinking and returned to the hooch for a night's sleep. I could dream about last night on that old mattress with Kim, heaven on earth.

When I returned to the hooch late the next morning after helping Maldonado with the morning ration pick up, Mooers was there waiting for me.

"Let's get going, Collins, the Captain's waiting for you."

"Well, how does it look? Man, you've gotta prep me for this. I don't want to go in cold."

"I told him just what you told me. If he buys it, you're in like Flynn; otherwise, you're fucked."

I took that as a grain of salt thinking of options if they were needed as we walked over to see the Captain. He got on me as soon as I walked through the door.

"So here's the hot shot who thinks he can come and go as his heart desires, fuck the rules and regulations of the US Army, fuck me, fuck the 1st SGT."

"You've got me wrong, sir." I preferred to never use that word but thought it prudent to get with the program at this point. Too much to lose. The "Sir" began again.

'I'm sick of you, Collins, you're running around the country like you own the place, hitchhiking all over hell, flying around on helicopters like you're some kind of fucking colonel; and you're just a goddamn private. You can go fuck yourself," said Captain Dewey. "I want your ass."

"I certainly understand, sir, that you have your own point of view, but my intentions were never more than to skip out for a few hours and visit with an old friend from home who happens to live twenty miles away. I realize I ought to have gone through channels but thought this might be simpler. It backfired on me, and here we are. Please understand I had no ill intent."

"Don't you realize, you fucking idiot, that in the army we have rules, and they must be adhered to. There is no flexibility, especially for a fucking private who thinks he's above the law. I should can you ass, mister. The thing is I was going to give you back your stripe. You're the only E-2 in the company and you've been over here longer than most of the other men. In fact, much longer than me. It's embarrassing to me to have a fucking E-2 Private in my company, period. Even so, you're not getting the stripe back till you're long gone from this place, I can guarantee you that. Furthermore, you're getting an Article 15 and fore fitting a month's pay. Keep in mind Private, any more fuck ups from you, and I'll see to it that you do a month in the Stockade. Now get the fuck out of here."

There are days in this world when things go fuck all ballistic…and there are days in this world when the biggest fuckups out there make out like a bandit. That's my kind of day…and this was one of them.

CHAPTER 16

I laid low for a couple of weeks after the run in with the CO, not so low that I didn't spend some long evenings in bed with Kim Lon, but what can you do. Matters of the heart prevail. At this point, at a late hour, I never returned to Long Binh through the main gate. The RMK-BRJ entry point for civilian workers was operating twenty-four hours with Vietnamese locals manning security. They always waved me through without the slightest problem. Otherwise, I might have had to back off seeing Kim Lon who was beginning to be for me the sweetest girl in the world. Tam Hiep was as always Off Limits, and I was "as always" AWOL, which was in reality a misnomer. Absent without leave would be more like going to Da Nang or Cambodia. Two hours in Tam Hiep is absent without a pass. They should institute a new classification AWOP, absent without pass. Makes sense to me.

Kim and I were lying on her bed once again soaked in sweat. Tam Hiep wasn't Phnom Penh, but it was still hot. More so after a vigorous, tender sexual workout, Kim seemed pensive.

"What we do, Collins, my friend, when you go? All GI go sometime."

At this point, I didn't care to go at all. I wanted to continue with her. My job with the mess truck was so simple that it was almost an enjoyable pastime. I was content.

"Will you leave me, Collin? We friend for long time now. Hoa think you her father."

That was food for thought. Life had rolled on for a time and then everything went to hell. I was beginning the procedure of being processed out of the company to 90th Replacement across the road. From there, it was to Bien Hoa and a 707 back to Oakland, even though I wasn't that keen on making the trip. I had told Kim Lon that it was possible I'd be back as a freelance photojournalist, which took a little dreaming, but what was I after all, but a dreamer. Some sort of publication would sign me on as a stringer I was fairly certain of, and then I'd return to Vietnam where I already knew the ropes. It was no problem for a civilian to fly from the States to Saigon for there were daily flights through Paris on Air France.

However, the process was going slowly. Captain Dewey had backed off but still maintained an edge regarding me. I'd mentioned earlier that my ETS was coming up and that shortly I'll be out of his hair forever.

I told him that "for the most part, we've gotten along well enough. You did your job and I did mine without a great deal of conflict.

"You think you got away with it, don't you, Collins? You might think not, but I noticed you. No insignia or rank on your fatigues, no company duty, no formations. For fuck all, the last few months, you've had your own truck and driver."

"Well, you know what, Captain, there's no sense wearing rank insignia when you have no rank. Let's face it, we're not the 1st Cav. or the 11th Armored Cav. or even the Big Red One that have great unit insignia. I'm not even sure what ours is."

"That's great, that's just fucking great. You call yourself a goddamn soldier and you don't even know what unit you're in." He let it go at that and indicated that he'd sign me out and be done with me. After he left, I asked Mooers who had listened to the whole tirade what he thought.

"You're good to go. Don't give it another thought. If something comes up, I'll let you know. Get a haircut and save him the trouble of getting pissed off the next time he sees you. He won't let you go without a good trim. The last revenge of the man who wields the power."

That night I ran into most of the boys down at the club drinking beer. Banks had done his time in the stockade and was also near his ETS, but of course, the thirty days in the lock up weren't good time, so he'd not be leaving till he'd made that up. Santimaw had been home on leave after extending for the six months in order to have that thirty-day leave at home. Unfortunately, he spent most of it in jail after getting into a bar fight. That was about par for him. I didn't remember Pacheco's position, so he filled me in.

"Wish I was going with you, Collins, but I just extended too. I can't go home so might as well stay here. I extended for six months too with a leave in France. Going to spend it on the French Rivera. Going to look up Bridget Bardot. I leave in another month."

The rest of the guys who remained that I hung around with had a matter of months left in country. I went back to my hooch early to think and sleep maybe. Another night and I'd skip out to see Kim Lon.

On the way out picking up the girls with Maldonado the next morning, we ran into Omar at the main gate.

"I looking for you, Collins, you should not go to Tam Hiep for few days. There will be trouble."

"What's going on, Omar?" I asked. "Kim hasn't said anything to me."

"She would now, but do not go there, I warn you. You will see. Stay in Long Binh. I have relatives in the North you know. I have to go now. Be careful."

I had no idea what Omar was talking about; however, Maldonado and I did keep our eyes open but saw nothing out of the ordinary. We finished up before noon, and I had a message to report to the orderly room.

"What's going on?" I asked Mooers as I walked in.

"You're out of here, fuckhead. Here're your papers. You're to take them along with your hand baggage and hoof it over to 90th Replacement. You know the place. It's not a mile away."

"I don't want to leave so soon. I haven't even said good bye to anyone here, much less Kim Lon. I can't leave now."

"You ass better be out of here before the Captain returns. I'd sign in there and find out how things work and then come back and see the boys and Kim Lon too if you want to chance one last run to Tam Hiep. That's my advice."

I decided I'd take it, shook Carl's hand, and left for the hooch to pack my bag. All that was in it was my old green uniform from Basic besides the usual personal things. I left everything else military here for the boys. I packed just what was necessary to make it back to Oakland for a discharge. I was done with the Army. However, I didn't forget my Miranda Cameras that I'd bought in the PX, still hoping at some point I could make it back here as a news person.

I walked out the back gate, crossed Highway 15 that ran to Vung Tau, and continued down the drive to 90th Replacement. There was a long line of GIs checking in to process out for transportation back to the States. That's all the troops leaving had to do. The incoming FNGs had to hang around till a slot was found for them In-Country. Us guys were finished.

It was after dark when they assigned me a tent; then I was put on guard duty in a bunker facing the Ammo Dump if you could believe it. How the hell could this happen? I'd have to leave in the morning early, to see the men in the old company area and hopefully somehow locate Kim Lon.

Within an hour, sporadic rifle fire could be heard in the distance. The SGT of the guard stopped by and requested any troops that were going home to come with him. He didn't want FNGs along that had no experience in Vietnam. A Spec-4 from the 25th and I left with him in a jeep, which headed immediately to the far side of the ammo dump main section facing the jungle that stretched nearly to Xuan Loc. There was a track unit already in position with three APCs that were visible to me. It wasn't at all apparent what we were to be doing considering the tracks appeared to be fully staffed.

"Ok, you two are to beef up this unit. Fill in wherever they need you," said the Sgt. "Whenever this lets up, check back in at Headquarters of the 90th to be rescheduled. This will probably blow over, so you shouldn't lose much time."

I was thinking then that I didn't mind being held up. This might give me time to check back in at the unit and possibly see Kim Lon. It appeared that the few rifle shots that we'd heard were probably just wild shots out toward the jungle. A low-key version of H & I, harassment and interdiction fire. Eventually, one APC was ordered to leave for II Field Forces, and we were to jump on top for the ride. If we ran into some VC, I wasn't sure what was expected, but we sure as hell didn't seem to be in a very good position.

Shortly after the track arrived at 11 Field Forces, we were ordered to beef up the guards along the wire that faced the main highway, a short distance north of my old main gate. The troops on the wire were from the 199th, Omar's unit just beyond these headquarters. Rifle fire was picking up. An RPG from the west side of the road made contact with another APC on the highway and blew it to hell. Some poor fuckers on that rig. Gunfire continued at a faster pace. At least one 50 Cal. was spewing out lead just below us, probably one that was mounted on a jeep or a deuce-and-a-half.

"I'm supposed to be done with this bullshit," said the guy from the 25th as tracers began edging toward us. We both opened up firing toward their source, joining the fray. "God damnit the fuck all. It ain't right this close to leaving. I've been in the middle of this kind of shit all year."

"Well, let's hope we're lucky. Keep your head down. I see a gunship coming in low, so we ought to be OK."

The gunship dropped down lower and fired off rockets into Widows Village, which was a short distance from the highway just across from II Field Force Headquarters, a perfect site to attack from. Whatever they hit burst into flames and incoming fire ceased toward us. We were receiving more reinforcements from the 199th. They'd be here in force to protect General Weyand, who commanded this, the largest corps command in Vietnam.

About then, the Ammo Dump blew. This was the largest yet of the three that I witnessed. It really did look like an atomic blast. A huge mushroom cloud filled the sky, and the shock wave really slammed us. The headquarters buildings were substantial, remaining undamaged, but I'd bet the tents in the company went down.

Then, Omar showed up.

"What the fuck's going on?" I asked him.

"Major attack. I warned you. I worry at gunships firing into Tam Hiep. I see some fire." Omar really did look worried. Ordinarily, he didn't take much seriously.

"Well, we can't get over there now, we'd get our asses shot off. Maybe in the morning."

It was late morning of the second day before we were able to leave. Buildings were smoldering from Tam Hiep to Ho Nai. Things didn't look good for the residents. I was worried about Kim Lon. But no matter what, she'd always been a survivor. We were given a ride to the 90th main gate, which gave me a chance to turn in the other direction and walk back in to the old company area. Indeed, it looked to be in turmoil but not much damage was visible. I walked over to the mess hall, not wanting to be seen at the orderly room. One of the boys ought to be around. I poured a cup of coffee and then Banks walked in.

"I thought you were fucking dead," he said, "or else on the freedom bird. You just disappeared."

I filled him in on my leaving from the orderly room and then on the happenings of the past two days. Then he began his side of the story.

"First, someone blew the KP truck. When Maldonado left for the run, all was quiet. Then there were rumblings of something in the works. A few shots, a few flares. All the civilians had disappeared earlier than usual, everyone of them, the fuckers. I told you they were all VC."

"OK, OK, but what happened to the truck?"

"Fini truck. Fini Maldonado. Deader than hell and half of the girls too. There was no way to figure out what or who did the deed."

"Where did it happen?" What a son of a bitch I was thinking. Those poor bastards.

"He was making the turn from Ho Nai down the main road out front here and the truck blew. Maybe the VC, or maybe a mistake. Friendly fire. No evidence either way. There were gunships operating in that vicinity. Either rockets or RPGs. I rode out with Bertzik to bring it in. The bodies had been cleared away; the wounded brought to the 93rd I believe, but who knows about that? They were all gooks."

Poor Maldonado, he almost made it. And the girls.

"Do you know if Hue made it, or if she was hurt or OK?"

"No, I don't" said Banks, "but you want to hear the rest of it?" I said of course.

"We don't know anything regarding the ammo dump detail. You heard it blow. A couple of the guys who came in said it's such a fucking mess there is no way of telling who or if any other men out there got it. It'll probably take a thorough roll call, but it's still too early for that. You can see that, can't you?"

Of course I could. I could see the possibility of just about anything. I asked what about the other guys, the rest of the company.

"All not elsewhere were on perimeter guard in the bunkers on the wire along Highways 1 and 15. As far as I know, this wasn't breached. You were just up the road at 11 Field Forces, so you're aware that elements of the 199th, the 9th and the 173rd pitched in at various points, so it doesn't appear they really got close enough to make a drive in. Maybe a few rounds of AK and a mortar or two. Who the fuck knows?" said Banks.

Between him and me, we had a handle on this comparatively small area. We'd wait for the Stars and Stripes for more detail. In reality, all that mattered to me now was Tam Hiep. It was still smoking. That was obvious. There was probably no way to approach it presently for either our military units or VC elements would prevent an attempt by me. In short, I was "too short" to attempt such short odds. I'd have to make it back to 90th Replacement to reinstate myself and check orders for departure. Anything else required some thinking and some sleep. I started walking down the road to the 90th, checked in amid a scene of almost complete chaos, found a bunk, and fell into a deep sleep.

My next memory was of a far-away sound of something clanging. It became louder as I came around from that deep sleep.

"Rise and shine, you assholes, you great warriors; formation in ten minutes," some jerk yelled as he rattled something on the metal bunks.

"A number of 'go fuck yourself's were heard, but we all climbed out to see what was up. Those of us who were leaving looking for a seat on a plane and those who had just arrived wondering and worrying about where the hell they'd be going. I was hoping to skip out after formation on the chance that it would be possible to make a last run to Tam Hiep. One last AWOL in my off-limits town. That, however, was never to be.

Me along with a dozen other troops with orders for the States were immediately loaded onto a Chinook for a flight to Cam Ranh Bay. The Bien Hoa airstrip was closed, so departure flights had been redirected there, and within hours, I was airborne for Oakland. My dreams of life with Kim Lon had been arbitrarily postponed, possibly forever.

CHAPTER 17

IT was two years beyond twenty when I next walked the trail to Tam Hiep. I was in no way AWOL, and this sad-looking village was no longer off-limits. However, as travel to Vietnam by US citizens was prohibited by the government, I was at the very least, sticking with the program. It was possible to pick up a visa in Bangkok and fly in on Air France.

For various reasons, I did not make it back to Vietnam before the war ended. Life intruded. It was many more years before I finally worked as a photo journalist, long after my Mirandas were obsolete, long after the marriages, the children raised and educated, a fortune made and lost.

In those earlier years before the embargo ended, Tam Hiep seemed not to have changed at all except for buildings. They were situated as before but were replacements, copies of a village long gone. The old people who lived there said that it had all been bombed and burned by the Americans during the last great battle, which had affected these parts. Like most of the buildings in the countryside that had been destroyed, it had been rebuilt.

I could not find a trace of Kim Lon. Her little house near the frog pond had not been rebuilt. Her picture produced scant recognition when presented. A few of the old people thought maybe but were not sure. Maybe they said. "Maybe I remember but she died during the bombing long ago. Maybe but I not sure. I do not know."

As the years passed, and I'd begun to travel to Iraq and Afghanistan for newspaper work, Vietnam also fit into the type of stories I wrote. Here's how it was so many years after the war. Some of the people from those times were still here, or back here. Sandy was running the old Kangaroo bar, now called just Bar #5. My cousin Emerson was back in Da Nang operating an NGO that built schools, countryside housing, clinics, and other such things. More importantly for me, I ran into Omar one day walking down Dong Koi St. the old Tu Do St. that was previously the Rue Catinat. He was hustling in front of the Caravelle Hotel.

"Omar," I yelled. "What the fuck man. How are you anyhow? I didn't think you'd still be alive."

We actually hugged before shaking hands. Omar was the closest human being on earth to my memories of Kim Lon from the time before. It took a long while for him to fill me in on those years since we'd seen each other. Having survived the fighting, he nearly made it out during the evacuation of Saigon by the US military. He'd climbed up the rear of the building and unfortunately found a full liquor cabinet and decided to take it home for a party and to return in the morning to catch a helicopter out with his family, then consisting of a wife, two sons, and an infant daughter. Poor Omar, he was one day too late.

We walked down to Bar #5 and ordered some beers. Sandy was the owner now, so it was a great time. However, I wanted to milk Omar about what happened to Tam Hiep after the fighting and, more importantly, what happened to Kim Lon.

"You know," said Omar, "I think Kim Lon is maybe some older than she tell you. Before the GI who father her child Hoa, Kim has very serious boyfriend name Quan. He VC with the Dong Nai Regiment."

"That can't be true, Omar. I knew Kim so well. She would not lie to me."

"For Kim, it not be lie. It is survival. I think Kim maybe just like the GI who she have baby with. I think she begin to love you. But other GI go. You go."

After getting used to the idea, I started thinking, and remembering. Remembering those times when Kim and the others who lived in Tam Hiep warned us about not visiting on certain days. For a few days, at various times. I remember unconsciously perhaps, most of us figured that they were all VC or at least sympathizers, that they were their people, not us. But for me, regardless of it all, a day had never passed over all those years without thinking of Kim Lon.

"Omar, I have traveled to Tam Hiep each time I come back to Vietnam and I can find no trace of what might have happened to Kim Lon. Someone must know something."

He thought for a minute and then said, "I can find out something. You remember I tell you before that my cousin is a Colonel in NVA. Now he is commander of PAVN unit stationed in Bien Hoa. They would have records of the Dong Nai Regiment. We can find out what happened to Quan from him. Maybe Kim disappear after Tam Hiep battle with Quan. Her house gone. Where else could she go? I can find out for you."

"If you can do that, Omar, I owe you my life…and much more beer." He laughed but agreed to look up his uncle tomorrow and find out anything he could about Quan, Kim's apparent longtime lover."

"All I can say, mate, is let it go. I've got a wife from Malaya and one from here and now am just looking for a girlfriend. Much easier, and there are many to choose from. They're all over the place, and they love foreigners who have money."

"Oh, well, Sandy, I'm just looking up an old friend. Hoping she made out alright after all's said and done. My last wife is on the lam, so who knows?"

We all drank up a number of times and shot the shit for the rest of the afternoon. So enjoyable, like so many years ago. I told Omar I'd meet him here tomorrow evening after he had time to speak with his cousin the colonel and see what he turned up.

"See you then" he said as he rode off in his Vespa. I walked back up the street to the Spring Hotel on Le Thanh Ton to catch a long night's sleep. This hotel had a great and early breakfast that went with the room, so I figured I'd get up at six and rent a Honda for a quick trip to Tam Hiep before the traffic built up. It'd been a few years now.

I made that trip to Tam Hiep the next morning, which wasn't productive or even that pleasurable. The traffic was impossible early on. Long Binh had been completely transformed by this time into a packed industrial park, mostly for foreign businesses looking for cheap labor. The entry to Tam Hiep was transformed into a military park with a large statue of a Vietnamese Long Range Patrol, soldiers from the local area. It was all cleaned up and quite pleasant, but it wasn't Tam Hiep. The old neighborhood that had been reconstructed was gone; hence, there was no one to try and talk with. I rode back hoping that Omar might turn up something. I could see now that the past was the past, up here in Tam Hiep as well as the whole fucking world.

Sandy was telling stories of the Aussie army in Vung Tau at Bar#5 when Omar walked in.

"My cousin knows," said Omar right off. "He has friend from the Dong Nai Regiment in his unit now who knew Quan. He thinks Quan did meet up with Kim Lon, but they both go to Hanoi many year ago. He think Quan get sick, but he does not know more about that. He think that today Kim be a famous artist. He say she have paintings in gallery up street from here. When we go I will talk them and see. OK, Private?" he said laughing.

Omar loved the idea that I was never more than a private. He was some kind of upper level Sgt. by the time he cashiered out of the ARVN. Lucky for him he never made it as an officer, for NCOs had to spend just one month in the re-education camps. Officers, maybe years.

We checked in at the gallery on the corner across from the Opera House on the possibility of Kim Lon having paintings on display there. It turned out she did. They looked like a Grandma Moses version of a Vietnam that wasn't working. The man at the agency had the address of a gallery in Hanoi he dealt with for a contact point. Nothing from her and the only thing about her that he knew of was that she was some kind of political dissident. That was more than enough for me. We thanked him and left. I thanked Omar, tipped him with a hundred-dollar bill, he always needed the money, and said my good byes.

My cousin Emerson Fitzpatrick, who had worked with IVS in Vietnam during the war, had returned to Da Nang and was running an NGO that was dedicated to rebuilding the country after almost continuous war from the end of the Second World War till Saigon fell in 1975. There was a lot of damage to fix to say the least and Emerson was back on the job.

Sections of Da Nang looked sadder than Saigon twenty years earlier, but progress was being made. Streets have been widened; the riverfront was getting cleaned up and converted into a park way. Much of the land between the river and the ocean was undergoing what appeared to be a kind of Vietnamese "urban renewal program," which showed great progress.

Emerson and I had a quick get together over lots of beer, talked of old times, and then returned to the NGO office, which doubled as his residence. He still slept in the back room. It must have been contagious. We drank the better part of a bottle of cognac and then directly passed into a deep sleep. I was in the air at seven o'clock headed for Hanoi with no idea at all of what to expect.

"Why you want to know where Kim Lon live?" asked the woman who ran the gallery in Hanoi where Kim displayed her paintings. I explained the whole story to her, and she finally gave me an address where she thought I'd be able to find Kim Lon, or at least learn where she might be located.

Her house was just a few blocks from Hoan Kim Lake, the quite beautiful centerpiece of downtown Hanoi. Only she wasn't in. The old woman there jabbered something to me that I could not understand at all. I found a kid on the street out front who spoke pretty good English and he helped. It turned out she was down in Thai Binh on the Red River Delta visiting a friend. After checking around, it seemed that Thai Binh was 100 klicks or so NE of Hanoi, maybe a couple of hours drive. I had no idea what the police situation might be in that area but figured to give it a try nonetheless. I'd come this far.

It took some doing but eventually I located a driver who spoke a smattering of English, and we were off. An hour or so along this road, and we passed the spot where the great photographer Bob Capa had been killed, stepping on a mine as he backed off the highway positioning himself for a picture, at the very end of the French Indo China War in 1954. Even today, I had no intention of walking around the countryside in an area I wasn't familiar with. In reality, all of Indo China was seeded with old ordinance of one type or another. Why take a chance?

Thai Binh wasn't a large town but still I had no idea where to find my old love. The driver said to write her name on a piece of paper, and he'd walk around talking with people and see what he could find out. Shortly, he came back with an address that wasn't five hundred feet from where we'd parked.

I walked up to the front door and knocked. And there she was, years older but still looking absolutely beautiful.

"Hi, Kim" I said. 'How are you?" She screamed and leaned against the door jamb to keep from falling. I stepped toward her to help keep her upright and she grabbed me and hugged hard as I did her. We said nothing for a few minutes and just held each other tightly. Eventually, she waved me in toward a chair and said she'd fix tea. I didn't know what to think. Her story from a burning Tam Hiep so many years ago, to here today in Thai Binh was probably heart breaking. She brought in the tea, and I asked her what had happened to her initially over the years. What had happened to Hoa? She was quiet for a spell; I think still getting used to the fact that I was there. That we were both alive and together after fifty years of not knowing.

"Who goes first, Kim, you or I." I asked. She smiled and began.

"I never tell you before that I have dear friend who VC, that I love. But he gone all the time and I meet you. After the other GI, I tell myself that I never be with GI again. But you come along, and it happen. You know the rest."

"When you left for the company back then, I think you come back soon to see me, but I never see you again. I wait in Tam Hiep for a week after the big battle but you no come back. My house gone, I don't know what to do. Then Quan come. The VC. My old friend that I love too. So I leave with him and stay with his family who live in the country north of Bien Hoa. I stay there till the end of the war in 1975. He have relatives in the North who arrange us to go there so I here since then. I never go back."

"What about your father?" I asked. "What happened with him?"

"I see him many times. In 1975, when Pol Pot take over Cambodia, he disappear in those years, and I never know what happen."

I told Kim how sorry I was to hear about her father and was hoping that Hoa had better luck.

"And what about Hoa?"

"Oh, Hoa very good. She grandmother now. She still teach school and have a good husband." I knew that must make Kim happy considering what might have happened.

I filled her in on my story since the day that Tam Hiep burned. The wives, the kids, Iraq and Afghanistan, what I was doing now, or rather what I wasn't doing now. She seemed to take it all in. I was most curious to know about Quan. What about him, and her.

"Quan save my live. He save Hoa. After the war when we come north many years, we are happy. I learn to paint and after long time can make some money with it. Now I make good money with it. But some of my paintings the government do not like. Unpatriotic they say. I don't care. I do what I do. So sometimes I have hard time from the government."

"But about Quan. Maybe ten years ago, he get sick. Doctor say he have cancer. He get from agent orange that the Americans cover much of South

Vietnam with. He die five years ago. I very sad for a long time but now OK. What can I do but keep living. I have Hoa and grandchildren and now have great grandchildren. I very lucky. I even have some money. Very lucky."

We sat there for an hour or so drinking tea, talking away about lesser things. I was curious about our days in Tam Hiep. Not so many days considering the time that's passed. I wondered where Quan stood, how each of us fit in.

"After I know you some time, I love two men. For me the more love the better and Quan cannot come very much. It very difficult for him to visit me and not have trouble. The VC regiment don't like him to leave and maybe the ARVN or the Americans catch him. Also he very tired all the time. Fighting day and night and not much food. But we stay in touch. You remember when I tell you to not come to Tam Hiep, it not be safe. He there with me why it not safe for you." She smiled some at that. Kim always had an impish side to her.

At this point, Kim mentioned that foreigners were not allowed in Thai Binh; the farmers revolt there, so they don't want word to get out about that. I'm thinking that it'd be best to hit the road too. Thus far, I'd been much luckier than I ever expected. Kim said her friend was coming back and that I'd best be going. She said she'd be back in Hanoi in two days and would get with me then. I told her I'd be at the Metropole. She could call or leave a message. That was our first meeting.

Kim did contact me at the Metropole, and for a few more days, we walked the streets of Hanoi getting to know each other once again. Old as we were. The last day I was there in Hanoi we were walking along the shores of Hoan Kim Lake, holding hands no less; two people in their later years remembering their long-lost youth. It occurred to me that there might be something more in this life…that there might be a future somewhere…with the Girl from Tam Hiep.

THE END